THE
FUGITIVE

THE
FUGITIVE

•

Pramoedya Ananta Toer

Translated by Willem Samuels

•

WILLIAM MORROW AND COMPANY
NEW YORK

First published in Indonesia in 1950 under the title *Perburuan* by Balai Pustaka Publishing. Reissued in Indonesia in 1954 and 1959.
English translation copyright © 1990 by William Morrow and Company, Inc.

Recognizing the importance of preserving what has been written, it is the policy of William Morrow and Company, Inc., and its imprints and affiliates to have the books it publishes printed on acid-free paper, and we exert our best efforts to that end.

Library of Congress Cataloging-in-Publication Data

Toer, Pramoedya Ananta, 1925–
    The fugitive : a novel / Pramoedya Ananta Toer ; translated by Willem Samuels.
        p.   cm.
    ISBN 0-688-08698-5
    I. Samuels, Willem. II. Title.
    PL5089.T8F84 1990
    899'.22132—dc20   89-28396
                                                                              CIP

Printed in the United States of America

First Edition

1 2 3 4 5 6 7 8 9 10

BOOK DESIGN BY NICOLA MAZZELLA

Note to the reader

The story of *The Fugitive* is set in the East Javanese town of Blora on the evening before and day of Japan's capitulation to the Allied Forces in World War II. Hardo, the main character, and his friend Dipo are fugitives from the Japanese military with which they had previously allied themselves in an effort to force the Dutch colonialists out of Indonesia and gain independence. Their rebellion against the dictatorial occupation forces six months earlier was doomed to failure when Karmin, the third conspirator, withdrew his support from the coup at the last minute. After months of being on the run, each additional hour brings the young men closer to capture and execution.

The novel begins with Hardo's attempt to visit his fiancée, Ningsih, on the day of her brother's coming-of-age celebration. Dressed liked a wandering beggar and half-starved from a self-imposed fast, Hardo will not reveal his identity to anyone, even his own father, for fear of endangering them and risking betrayal. Hardo's relationships with both his own father and the father of his fiancée form an important element in the book; the ambiguity of their relationship, a balance of love and cruelty, is a recurring theme in Pramoedya's writing.

Though *The Fugitive's* structure follows the general outline of the traditional Javanese shadow-puppet play, it is nonetheless a novel of contemporary and nationalistic spirit.

Pramoedya wrote *The Fugitive* while at Bukit Duri Prison, a forced labor camp, where he was imprisoned from 1947 to 1949 for his active role in the Indonesian revolution that followed the end of World War II.

THE
FUGITIVE
·

ONE

The final sounds of the gongs of the bronze orchestra faded in the evening air. That morning the son of the subdistrict chief of Kaliwangan had been circumcised. Guests had gone home and now came the murky light of twilight. The only visitors remaining were a band of beggars looking at the area where the shadow play had earlier been performed. The beggars, men and women both, were almost naked. The men covered only their genitals. While some of the beggars squatted on the ground, others leaned against the pillars that supported the roof of the three-sided pavilion where the festivities had taken place. The floor was only two centimeters higher than the ground.

Among the group of beggars was a young man

whose ribs and breastbone, like those of the other beggars, stood out like the keys of a xylophone. His arms
were thin, his stomach shrunken, and his legs little more
than a pair of walking sticks. Yet he was different from
the other beggars. Unlike the others his eyes did not
roam the area but remained focused on the newly circumcised boy who sat lounging on an antique settee. The
young beggar remained completely motionless, his body
as rigid as a nail. With his bony left arm, he clung to one
of the pillars. His only item of clothing was a loincloth.

Whenever someone from the main house came out
to the pavilion to clean or pick up, a chorus of moans
erupted from the beggars' mouths. Even so, the pallid
choir failed to attract attention, and no sooner had a servant completed his task than he would leave again. The
young beggar's mouth remained firmly closed. He stood
stiffly, with his left hand clutching the pillar.

The circumcised boy at whom the beggar stared sat
alone, the lower part of his body covered in a brown
sarong. The smile on his face gave him the appearance of
a primary school student who had just passed his final
exams. But when his eyes caught sight of the beggar's
stare, their light faded. The small pine branch, a switch
that he held in his hand, moved incessantly as if he were
trying to shoo away flies. The boy's eyes moved from the
beggar to the silent orchestra and the frozen row of
shadow puppets standing before the dark screen.

No lamps flickered in the dusk. In Blora the poor
people generally kept their lamps burning very low. The
red light of the sun floated in the deep blue sky and the
two colors finally mixed into one. The dark green wrappers from sweets that lay scattered on the ground turned
to gray. Yellow banana peels became brown and young
coconut leaves took on an ochre cast.

An older woman emerged from the house and approached the circumcised boy. She spoke to him affectionately. "Would you like anything, Ramli?"

The boy shook his head silently but pointed his fir branch at the beggars. The woman looked to where he was pointing. "Why don't you give them something, Mother?" he asked her. "Why do you let them stand there, waiting?"

The boy's mother glared at the beggars, who had gathered in search of handouts. "These days, there are thousands of them around. They're like ants. And if you pay them any mind at all . . ."

The boy stopped to lay the branch on his lap. "But if you're not going to give them anything, why do you let them wait there?"

"Why not? They'll tire soon enough of waiting and leave by themselves," she told him. The boy played with his fir fan, now black in the evening light. He stared at the ground and tapped his feet. "Don't move your legs," his mother reminded him. "It'll take longer to heal." She then left him and walked to the edge of the pavilion.

As she stepped in front of the beggars, the woman stopped and puffed out her chest. She stood there watching them, pulling her body straight and thrusting her narrow chin forward. Wisps of hair fell across her temples. Her nostrils flared as she raised her arm and jabbed her finger through the air. In a voice almost loud enough for a scream she began to shriek: "You bunch of monkeys! Get out of here! Go! You stink to high heaven. Go on, get out!"

As she spoke, there rose like a church choir the sound of both male and female voices. "Ma'am, ma'am, take pity on us, ma'am."

The choir soon broke into a litany of separate cries. The beggars blinked as if just waking from sleep. As if they were Japanese, they bowed their bodies before her.

Seven pairs of skinny arms reached upward. Flies buzzed around their scabby skin. The one beggar remained motionless, not moving and not saying a word.

The woman's feet stayed firmly rooted on the ground. "Get out!" she barked as she jabbed her index finger at them again.

The voices of the weak choir rose again. "Take pity on us, ma'am, please . . ."

The one beggar did not move. For a moment he stared wanly at the woman but then let his eyes search the room until they rested once more on the circumcised boy. The beggar's thick black hair fell below his shoulders. His eyes hung deep inside their hollows. His eyebrows were bushy and unkempt.

"Mother," the boy called from his place on the divan.

"Get out of here, all of you!" the woman roared again before she turned around and walked back to the boy. "Yes? What is it?" she asked sweetly.

"I want you to give them something," the boy said weakly.

The woman hesitated. "Is that going to be your gift today? Is that what you want?"

"Yes, that's all I want." The boy paused for a second before continuing. "When is Hardo coming back?"

"Shhh! You're not to mention that name around here," his mother warned as she returned to the main house. "I'll get something for them," she said as she disappeared behind the shadow screen.

At the edge of the pavilion the beggars hovered together as before. With the sun setting in the west, the pavilion was growing dark. The night wind began to blow softly, and from the outdoor kitchen beside the house came the sound of people cooking. The palm branches that decorated the doorways and the paper streamers that climbed through the air from the rafters to the roof of the pavilion swayed gently back and forth. A gecko lizard called twelve times.

"Mother," the boy called to his mother as she appeared with a basket of cakes in her hand. "Mother!" he said more insistently.

"What is it, Ramli?" the woman asked as she approached.

The boy pointed at the solitary beggar. The woman's eyes followed her son's hand. "Who is that?" he whispered.

"What do you mean, who? You ask the strangest questions sometimes. Who else if not some lazy bum from the back woods?"

"But he looks like . . ."

"Who does he look like?" she demanded.

"Like . . . Hardo."

The boy's comment angered her as the tension in her body returned. "Stop imagining things," she hissed under her breath. "If someone were to hear you, you could get the whole lot of us in trouble." She walked to the edge of the pavilion with the basket hanging from the crook of her left arm. With her right hand she divided the cakes among the beggars. "Now, once and for all, go away," she warned them.

In return for her alms she received a chorus of muted thanks, but the one beggar remained still and silent. Not raising a hand to accept the offering, his deep-set eyes stared at the woman in front of him. One by one the other beggars left and soon he was standing alone.

The woman looked at him with surprise. "What is it? Why don't you take this and go?" she muttered.

He didn't answer.

"Mother," the boy called from his chair. She turned her head to look at him. "He looks like Hardo."

The woman's brow furrowed as she looked again at the beggar in front of her. "Go!" she insisted, stamping her foot. Her eyes studied the beggar from his feet to his forehead. He took his left arm from the pillar and the woman noticed on the back of his right arm a long thin scar lighter in color than his skin. She blinked rapidly. Her body stiffened as she screamed, "Hardo!" before she slapped her hand on her mouth. As she stood transfixed, the beggar suddenly bowed and left.

Evening's darkness had come quickly. The air felt clean once more. Swallows flitted back and forth on the currents of the gentle wind. Here and there, across the landscape, the dim lights of kerosene lanterns grew brighter, like stars in an ashen sky. The night air filled with the sound of drums in mosques—it was time for evening prayer—and small children crying.

The beggar walked listlessly, his eyes on the ground before him. Ten, then fifteen houses retreated behind him. One foot forward, then the next; his bone-thin arms hung weakly at his sides. He arrived at the village road that led to the city. Stretching out on either side were rice fields which now, between seasons, had been planted with other crops.

"Karmin, Commander Karmin, where are you now?" the beggar whispered to himself, and then fell silent. Head bowed, he continued on.

The moon had yet to rise and stars flickered calmly above a procession of clouds. Kaliwangan, a village on the outskirts of the small city of Blora, was peaceful. The rutted twilight road was almost empty. Save for the beggar, there were only one or two other people about. There were no cows or buffalo. He walked forward, following a straight path, in the direction of the city. Crickets began to trill their song, the only song they knew. Bats swept through the air like children's kites in frantic competition.

From somewhere behind the beggar came the sudden sound of hurried footsteps. The beggar did not turn. He continued walking forward, his head fixed firmly on the ground.

"Ningsih, where are you?" he whispered softly before falling into silence again. The sound his fingers produced as he scratched himself was like sandpaper. "Karmin! Commander Karmin!" he whispered. "I didn't think it possible of you. When will we meet again? Ningsih," he moaned, "why weren't you at home? It's been half a year now. How did I manage to survive? How did I survive the darkness of Sampur Cave? Oh, God, it was so dark in there. And so quiet too. And you weren't there . . ." He continued walking. Every so often he looked upward to stare at a star that flickered through the moving clouds. For a moment it was visible, then it was gone. "Where is it?" he asked himself. "The one that witnessed our promise? It's gone, Karmin! I've lost it as I lost you in your betrayal." He walked onward. "It's gone," he whispered again. "Gone, just like you."

The sound of footsteps grew closer. The beggar turned abruptly to the left and entered a cornfield to sit in meditation among the stalks. He lowered his head deeply into his lap. Above him hovered the twilight's darkness. He sat motionless five meters from the edge of the road.

On the road a short thin figure came into sight: a man walking fast, his white robes fluttering in the darkness, grumbling audibly to himself. "Him again, him again! Everyone had forgotten about him but now he's back!" he swore under his breath. "It's him again. How come my wife misses him so much? And Ramli too? And now I'm supposed to find him. You fool," he rebuked

himself. "What's the rush?" He stopped speaking, and as
he slowed his pace his robes fell to his sides. He stepped
to the edge of the road and lowered his body to relieve
himself. Behind him, in the field, the beggar sat in meditation. The older man picked up his grumbling where he
had left off. "Fool! What's the rush? It would be better to
sit here for half an hour. Take the easy way out and go
back to the house and accuse my wife of lying. Say
Hardo was nowhere to be found. I'll pretend I'm angry
about getting tired and sweaty." He laughed, pleased
with the thought.

He pulled a flint and tinder from his pocket. As he
struck the flint the spark outlined his face in the darkness.
"Damn tinder! It must be wet! Why won't it light?" He
stood and crossed the road. He struck the flint again.
Sparks flew and the vague lines of his wide nose and pro-
tuberant eyes emerged. Finally the tinder caught fire. He
lit a cigarette and began to smoke.

"What's Hardo doing here anyway?" he cursed.
"Where did he get the nerve to come back to Blora? And
looking like a beggar, no less, or so my wife said. What
in the world can you hope for from a beggar? He'd just
waste my money, that's what! I'm sure that's what he
would do." He took a drag of his cigarette but then his
irritation rose. "No word of him all this time and now
he's back here stirring up trouble. He'll have the Japanese
calling people up and marching them out and ordering
them to scour the mountains around Blora. That search
for him in Plantungan really had people stirred up. I
mean, for God's sake, the Japs had everyone terrified.
What a godforsaken day that was. An awful day! My legs
felt like they were going to drop off. I for one wish he'd
been caught. How in the world did he escape? There
must have been a thousand people after him and he still
got away."

He silently smoked his cigarette and then muttered some more. "Maybe he does have secret powers," he said with a trace of worry. "There were four thousand people out there. What a pitiful end his father had, the chief of Plantungan. Fired from his job and the government seizes his property besides. And then his wife goes and dies. Dead from grief, I suspect. From Allah we come and to Allah we must return." Taking another drag from his cigarette, he began to cough. The glowing butt fell from his lips to the ground. "Can you believe it? His father fired . . ."

On the horizon the clouds had disappeared and the stars flickered dimly. The village road stretched hazily in the direction of the city. Kaliwangan was a darkened mass dotted with candles like stars in a cloudy sky. And in the city, beyond a grove of bamboo that moved restlessly with the wind, the lights of street lamps appeared and disappeared.

The beggar sat in silence, his hands on his calves. Before him, not too far away at all, sat the grumbling man in white, the glow from his cigarette brightening and dimming with the movement of his lips. The beggar heard every word the man said. He slowed his breathing and silently scratched himself. He smiled wistfully, then whispered to himself, "What a complainer. He hasn't changed a bit."

"And what was Ramli going on about? If Hardo really is a beggar, why should he care about him? Imagine, a filthy beggar! That's all it seems the Japanese have given us: their disgusting snails and beggars. What in the world could have gotten into Ramli's head? Here we put on an entire shadow play for him and he can hardly smile. I haven't the foggiest idea what he really wants. Why didn't he ask me for a bicycle? If he asked for one with pneumatic tires, I would have bought it for him.

Hell, Ong wanted to sell me one yesterday. But no, Ramli didn't want anything. He didn't ask for anything. And then when that beggar arrives he comes out with this crazy request. It's crazy, that's what it is. He wants a beggar! Now isn't that a crazy request? 'Father, find Hardo for me,' he asks. Damn, if he really is a beggar then why would I want to bring him home! And then his mother goes on about it too. How could anyone love a beggar? Shit, a dead chicken is worth more than a beggar. If there were a dead chicken on the road, people would fight for it. But a dead beggar? They'd all run off and hide, afraid they might have to do some work." He paused, cleared his throat, and began to smoke again.

The beggar sitting behind him listened carefully to the man's complaints. Feeling cold, he crouched and hugged his knees tightly together. Slowly he shifted the weight of his skeletal frame to the left and then scratched his long, matted hair.

"I imagine the guests are on their way," the man griped. "Guests . . . what kind of guests are they anyway? Now, under the Japanese, guests are beggars, every single one of them. And they're blind too. They know the Japanese are going to steal their crops, even though there's not a single Japanese stationed in the village, but they won't lift a finger to steal them back. Guests? What good do they do me? At most, the Chinese guests might help a little. But, what the hell; I'm not hurting. At least I have my teak and can take as much from the Japanese as I want."

The cigarette that glowed in his lips lit up the man's coarse and frowning features. Finally, he pulled his body upright and began to walk off in the direction of the city. Slowly the beggar stood and followed. Through the evening's silence the beggar could hear the strains of "Megatruh," a mournful song of sadness and displeasure.

"When will we meet again, Karmin?" the beggar whispered and then began to speak softly between the bars of the song the man ahead of him sang. "Is that the kind of man your father is, Ningsih? I feel sorry for you if it is, for a man such as that could have no idea of your feelings." He scratched his buttocks and then his head. "And you, Karmin, you must come back to me. Don't worry; I will not seek revenge for your treachery."

As the two men walked, the wind gathered force. The stars above flickered, pale yellow in the deep blue of the sky. Clusters of bamboo at the base of the darkened sky, a fence for the city beyond, swayed back and forth. Between the bamboo poles the street lamps played a game of hide and seek.

When the older man with the cigarette suddenly stopped, the man behind him stopped too. And as the first man turned around, the latter swiftly lowered his body to sit at the edge of the road with his feet in the dry rice field.

"Should I keep looking or not?" the old man wondered aloud. "All that guy does is give me trouble. Well, you just wait. Soon you won't be making more trouble for anyone," he threatened. "The guests must be there by now. How long have I been gone? Ten minutes? Half an hour?" As if changing his mind about something, he turned completely around and began to walk back in the direction of the village, but no sooner had he gone a hundred meters when he turned again and retraced his steps toward the city. As he passed the squatting beggar, he grumbled again, "That's the trouble with trying to please your wife. It's ridiculous! Here I am, the chief of Kaliwangan, and my wife has me scouting for a beggar. But I couldn't have anyone else do it. That might really get me in trouble." His voice faded as he proceeded farther down the road. He walked slowly, with the glowing butt of his cigarette swinging in the darkness. "Anyone could go and tell the Japanese that the headman of Kaliwangan is in contact with platoon commander Hardo. And then what would happen? I'd have my head cut off, that's what would happen. Well, it's a good thing he is a beggar." Five meters beyond the beggar, he stopped. "And having the nerve to come around looking for Ningsih! He'd be better off . . ." The southern wind carried his words away. He contemplated the road ahead. When the wind slackened he started to walk again. The beggar rose to follow. "The Japanese would have my head, no doubt about that. It will be a happy day for me when I hear he's dead and has been eaten by maggots. At least I won't have to worry about Ningsih anymore. Ningsih, oh Ningsih, you're such a fool to wait for him. Your misguided loyalty is foolishness. I can't believe it. She wouldn't even come home for Ramli's circumcision. 'I have my work and my memories to attend to.' That's what she said." He stopped and threw his cigarette butt into the rice field, then turned around and walked back in the direction of the bluish-black village.

The beggar immediately settled himself beside the road again. The man, almost beside him now, suddenly stopped and looked down as he saw the figure of the man seated beneath him.

The beggar intentionally breathed louder.

"Good grief!" The older man jumped back. "Is that a man? Oh, heavens, that gave me a start."

The beggar gave no response.

"It is a man, isn't it?"

Receiving no answer, the man felt the human pile with his hands. The beggar said nothing, even as his chest rose and fell with his breath.

"My God, it is a man. I'm sorry," he apologized, "I'm old and my eyes aren't very good." He felt the beggar's arms. "Yes, there should be a scar on his left arm. No, just a second, the right arm. Yes, it's the right arm that has the scar. Ah, this is the right arm. And this is the scar of a Japanese bayonet. I remember that very well. Is that you, Hardo? Is it really you?" He sat down beside the beggar. "You poor man. Such a shame!"

The night progressed, second by second. Neither of the two men spoke. The wind picked up again and the bamboo, the city fence, rustled and swayed in the wind. Rays of lights darted through the bamboo poles, like fireflies in pursuit.

"How did you ever get to be in such a state?" the old man asked.

The beggar wheezed and the sound of his breath was like wind from a blowpipe.

"Have you been sitting here long?"

The beggar said nothing.

"My wife and I would like you to come to the house. That's why I came after you. At first I thought they were lying because we hadn't heard a word about you for so long. But you're all right, aren't you?" He waited for an answer but the beggar remained close-mouthed. "We've had no real news about you for half a year, just rumors is all. But you're all right, you're safe, aren't you?" Again he waited for a response, but the beggar said nothing. "I'm sorry, son, but my eyes aren't very good anymore. My sight's so bad, I can't really see how you are. But come home with me, Hardo." The beggar said nothing. The old man sighed. "But I'm afraid if you do come home"—his voice wavered—"Ningsih won't be there. She's living in the city now. She moved to the city about a half a year ago too, right after the Japanese started hunting for you. Yes, she's living in the city now. That's where she is."

"And now," the beggar mused, "will you try to have me arrested again?"

"Arrested?" the old man shrieked. "May lightning strike me dead if I should do such a thing, I swear."

"There's no need to swear. I saw with my own eyes how you came looking for me in the mountains around Plantungan. I saw you, with my own two eyes."

"Hardo, please. You don't know how much pain it caused me to have to carry out the Japanese order but it was the Japanese who appointed me chief of Kaliwangan, you know. And they loaded us all onto trucks and ordered us to look for a man with a long scar on his right arm." He fished in his pockets for something. "And didn't Ningsih swear at me for that. She had no kind words at all for her poor father. She said to me, 'So, to keep your job, you're going to hunt for Hardo?' She actually said that." He paused. "Well, I didn't know what to do. I mean, those were the orders. But what I told Ningsih was this. I told her, 'Even if Hardo is in front of my eyes, I will not see him!' As it turns out, I didn't see you. All those people looking and no one could find you." He spoke softly. "They couldn't find you. It was a miracle. You know, don't you," he enthused, "that the people hold you in high regard for what you did. Everyone, without exception, thinks highly of you. And I even more than the rest. People say that you must have special powers. I wonder, is that true?"

The beggar sighed.

"You used to be so talkative. Now you won't say anything at all. What's wrong, Hardo?"

The beggar sighed again.

"You poor man. You've been through so much. Too much, I say. And no clothes. No shoes and you're the son of a district chief. Listen, what would you think if I were to give you my clothes to wear?"

"That's not necessary."

"But you have nothing."

There was a long silence before Hardo finally answered. "No."

The headman spoke as if to himself. "Everything is different now. Your father . . ." He paused to change his course of conversation. "Ramli misses you. He won't go to the mosque anymore for his lessons. What's to become of him? I've given up trying to think of what to do. I really don't know what to do, Hardo. You're the only one he'll listen to. You always used to give me advice on the children but now, with you gone, Ramli won't listen to me anymore. Every day, all he asks is 'Where's Hardo, Father?' or 'Where's Hardo, Mother?' And it's difficult because you can't fool him anymore. He knows the Japanese are after you. If he hadn't just been circumcised, I'm sure that he himself would have run after you. That I'm sure of. It's a good thing he was circumcised. If not, I don't know. . . . So, anyway, I hope that you'll come home with me. Please?"

"Thank you all the same."

The village chief drew a deep breath. "You wouldn't have to stay for long. Just a little while would do."

"No."

"Only God the Most Powerful knows how much I'd like to have you beneath our roof once more. Why does it seem that all the things you used to like you have no mind for anymore?" His voice was softly pleading. "I remember that first time how pleased you were to see our garden and the fish pond set in the shade beside the bamboo grove and the vegetables you liked and the fat young goats . . . and I remember how after you'd come home from a walk with Ningsih through the estate . . ." He stopped as if remembering something. "But Ningsih doesn't live at home anymore. She wouldn't be there to walk with you through the grounds. Ever since the Japanese started hunting you, she's been in the city. Oh, I'm repeating myself, aren't I? I told you that already. Poor Ningsih, it would be such a shock for her to see you in this condition."

"Mmmm."

"Won't you come back to the village with me?"

"No thank you."

"Please," the village chief urged.

"Mmmm."

"Why won't you say anything? Maybe you've stopped thinking of me as your father. Maybe I'm not good enough for you anymore."

The beggar laughed weakly. A cluster of clouds passed over the horizon and he looked up at the sky. "That star . . ." he whispered but did not continue. He bowed his head again.

"What star?" the village chief asked. "What do you mean, 'That star'?" he asked again. "I heard Ningsih say the same thing once. And when I asked her about it, all she said was that the star that was now covered by clouds would reappear tomorrow. I remember her saying that because it rained hard that night and in the middle of the night, Ningsih must have been dreaming about stars or something because in her sleep she kept saying, 'That star, that star . . .' No, I haven't forgotten that," he coughed and cleared his throat. "What in the world am I talking about that for?"

The beggar's soft laugh held a trace of mockery. He scratched his armpits and head.

"Come on home, Hardo. Mother is waiting."

"No thanks."

"What's wrong? What are you afraid of? There's no one who's going to betray you. Who would dare? In fact, everyone would offer you shelter. Didn't you yourself once comment on how terribly the people are suffering! Indeed they are and they think of your rebellion against the Japanese as an expression of their own feelings. It's true, Hardo, and no matter if someone were to see that scar on your arm, he still wouldn't say anything." He tried to speak more convincingly. "No, no one would betray you. If you're that unsure, you could stay inside. You wouldn't have to show your face at all. Come home with me. I give you my promise. I'll take responsibility for your safekeeping. I'd risk my neck for you, just like Sumo did when he hid that Australian soldier. You can take a bath and get some sleep. I know we have lots of guests tonight but don't worry about that; they wouldn't be a problem. They wouldn't recognize you. We could go in through the back door. Come on. Won't you come home with me?"

"No thanks."

Silence surrounded the two men before a brace of night birds volleyed a song above their heads. But a moment later, silence returned.

"Don't you want to talk to me anymore?" The old man waited for a reply. "Are you afraid that I'll turn you in?" He still received no answer. "You don't have to worry. I might work for the Japanese. I mean they appointed me to my position but I would never betray anyone, especially you; after all, you're like my own son. May lightning strike me dead if I were to have any thought of betraying you. I'm serious. Trust me. It's not as if we're strangers. You know me. You can come home with me. Please." He waited again for an answer.

"No thank you, one thousand times no thanks."

The old man sighed. "Only the Prince in Heaven knows how much I long for you to come home with me and for you to leave this kind of life behind." The night wind felt cool. "Aren't you cold?" he asked.

"No."

"Wouldn't you like to put on these clothes of mine?"

"No."

Again there descended an uneasy silence, then the sound of a cricket's trill. The village headman cleared his throat. "You used to smoke. You always had a clove cigarette hanging from your mouth. That's right, Scissors brand cigarettes as I recall. I have some with me. Would you like one?"

"No."

Silence reigned once more. The clouds now bordered the horizon. In the village a gong sounded once, just once, but was soon followed by a roll of drums. "The vendors must have arrived. And it's not even eight o'clock. Won't you please come home to see Ramli?" Receiving no answer, the village chief continued to speak in a voice that begged for understanding. "Ramli wants to see you. If you don't want to stay long, you don't have to. A little while will do. His mother would like to see you too. Ever since that awful incident six months ago, both of us have prayed for your safety, your good health, and your freedom from the Japanese. All of us waited for news from you. And now that you're here wouldn't it be strange for you not to visit? Won't you come home?"

The beggar's forced cough signaled his doubt about the chief's words. He scratched his back.

"Ramli has something new to show you," the chief said proudly. "He's learned how to make soap from ashes and coconut oil. A couple of weeks before his circumcision he made a bunch of it for us. And you remember the well near the garden fence, don't you? It is still an endless source of water for us. And Ningsih made a special place for you to sleep. No one else has ever slept there. Except your father, that is. He stopped by the other day to see Ramli before his circumcision. He said to me, 'It scares me to think of where Hardo might be. He must be suffering.' Don't you want to see your father, Hardo?"

"No," the beggar answered.

"Are you sure?"

"Mmmmm."

"But your father would like to see you." The old man shifted the conversation once more. "You should see the patch of corn you planted. Wouldn't you like to see that? After you left Ramli planted some hot pepper bushes and now the garden is covered with red. The peppers are enormous. Wouldn't you like to see them?"

"No."

"What would you like to do?"

Hardo paused in thought for a moment before speaking in a slow but forceful voice. "Has Karmin ever stopped by?"

The old headman hesitated before he spoke. "Oh, he's been around about twice a month since the Japanese started looking for you. He always asks about you."

"And what do you tell him?"

"Well, because I myself don't know, I just tell him that I don't know. He says that what you did was the mark of a true hero." The beggar laughed weakly in disbelief. "And before he comes," the village chief continued, "he always stops at Ningsih's house in the city to ask her to come with him."

"Where is Ningsih now?" the beggar quizzed.

The old man seemed unsure of his own answer. "In the city."

"The city?" the beggar asked suspiciously. "The city?" He took a deep breath and retreated once more into silence.

"Yes, in the city," the village chief whispered. He struck his flint and lit another cigarette. The cigarette made crackling sounds as it burned. The thick nose and protruding eyes of the headman reappeared in the cigarette's glow. "Like to smoke?" The question received no reply. "Don't you smoke anymore?" Waiting for an answer, the old man puffed on his cigarette but still found no reply. "I guess you don't care for any of the things you used to like. Doesn't seem so, anyway. Don't you remember the dark green pepper plants with their bright red fruit? And a good cigarette to warm your body? The fish pond with its green and mossy water and the cornfield as it rustles in the wind? Wasn't it only four months before the Japanese started looking for you that you dug that pond? And wasn't it you who stocked the pond with young fish? Remember how Ningsih used to go down to the pond to feed the fish bran? The fish are big now. Wouldn't you like to see them and to breathe in the fresh air? You always said how you enjoyed the view from there. And the delight you took in the animals you saw! Won't you come home with me?"

"No."

"No? I guess I don't know anymore what it is you like. The pond is absolutely teeming with fish but Ningsih says, 'No one is to touch them.' And so it has been just as when you left. We haven't caught a single fish out of there. And Ningsih—"

"Where is Ningsih now?" the beggar interrupted.

"In the city," the village chief answered, displeasure evident in his voice.

"Where in the city?"

"The city is all. With another teacher from the Kartini School."

"Oh." The beggar breathed deeply.

The headman continued to smoke, and each time he drew on his cigarette his pronounced features emerged from the dark. "And a day after that failed search for you, the Japanese military unit leader, your unit leader, came to the village with Karmin to ask me about you. That was a frightening experience. His face was so red he looked like he was drunk. And he never stopped shouting in that language of his. They checked the bureaus and armoire and read all the papers they found. All of them. They even looked under the beds, in the loft, and the rice barn too. And the officer, with that red nose of his—I'll never forget that beet-red nose—and with his almost unintelligible way of speaking, said to me something like, 'You watch it, you, if you hide a traitor here, understand?' Then he hit his neck with the side of his hand and said, 'Our police, you understand? The military police. Do you know our police?' I nodded and he said, 'Very good. Your head get cut off, you understand?' Then he started to question me about Ningsih. 'Where is his fiancée?' he asked. And that's when my whole body started to shake. It was Ningsih I was worried about. They were going to go off to find her too. I was frightened, Hardo. I had lost you and I thought I was going to lose Ningsih too."

The beggar cleared his throat. The calm of the evening returned as the wind died; even the crickets stopped their trilling.

"So then what?" the beggar asked.

"So I told them, 'In the city.'"

"Where?"

"Just in the city." The old man hesitated. "And then they left in their automobile. The officer's nose was still red, but before they left Karmin whispered to me, 'Don't worry, I'll take care of Ningsih. But be careful and don't say anything about this. If you don't follow my advice, the consequences could be most unfortunate. Keep that in mind and don't forget that I am a soldier.' I couldn't think of anything to say. And after that the two of them left."

"Platoon Commander Karmin . . ."

"And since that time, he's been here often. He stops in for a little visit and then he's off again."

Silence returned. The sound of a gong floated through the night.

"The shadow play has begun," the beggar remarked.

"Not yet," the chief answered. "That's still the vendors. The show won't begin for another hour. Let's go home, Hardo." The old man waited for a reply as he drew on his cigarette but an answer never came. As he took another puff his wrinkled features became a scowl. He flicked the cigarette butt in front of him and it fell beneath a vine. Suddenly, as if remembering a question he hadn't thought of before, he asked, "How are you, anyway?"

"Fine."

"Fine? Like this, you're fine?" He waited for the beggar to say something but the man remained silent. "Do you like the way you are? Don't you want something different?"

"No," the beggar said firmly.

"Then I don't understand at all. Why have you changed so? You don't like any of the things you used to like. You're completely different now. I think of you in your smart green uniform with your stripes and sword, standing in position beside a Japanese officer and getting in and out of staff cars. But that's all gone. The fish pond, the garden . . . you don't care about them anymore. I don't understand. Really, I don't understand." He exhaled grandly. The glow of the cigarette butt on the ground beneath the creeper dimmed beneath its thin cover of ash. He spoke slowly, as if remembering something. "Ramli and his mother want you to come home but you don't want to. Why won't you? Oh, Prince of Heaven, I tried. I did follow him but my son would not return. If Ningsih were there, she'd make sure you came home. But . . ."

"Where is she?" the beggar whispered.

"The city." The chief hesitated. "The city."

"But where?"

"With her friend from the Kartini School," the old man stammered.

Now it was the beggar's turn to speak, but in the end he said nothing. The headman steered the conversation in another direction.

"Are you able to manage in the condition you're in?"

"Yes."

"You are? That, I do not understand at all." The old man spoke as if to a child. "When you go to the city you see children sprawled lifeless at the side of the road. In front of the market and the stores, down beneath the bridge, on top of garbage heaps and in the gutters there are corpses. Nothing but corpses. The place is filled with the dead—children and old people. And you know what they do? If they're going to die, before they take their final breath, they first gather together a pile of teakwood or banana leaves that have been used to wrap food in. And they cover their bodies with those leaves and then they die. It's like they know that in two hours they're going to die and that after they're dead no one is going to prepare them for burial. These are crazy times we're going through. And I don't know why it is. In all my life this is the first time I've seen anything like it. Corpses. Wherever you go, unattended corpses. Come home, Hardo."

"Thank you but no." Hardo discounted the old man's plea.

"No one will betray you." The old man stared at the fading glow of his cigarette butt. The stem of the creeper that had been outlined in the dark was no longer visible. Finally, the glow died.

"Are you afraid someone will turn you in?"

"No."

"Then why won't you take my offer of a nice place to stay? You used to like it there."

The beggar chuckled.

"Aren't you afraid of dying like this?"

Hardo now laughed. In the starlight the village chief watched Hardo's body shake, but he said nothing. "Afraid?" Hardo posed. "Do you know what it is that makes a man afraid? What makes a man a coward? It's greed. Once a person has reduced his needs to the absolute minimum, he has no more reason to fear. He need not be afraid of anything or anybody."

"I don't understand what you're saying," the chief sighed. "All I see is that you're having a hard time. That you're suffering and in a great deal of pain."

"But that's your point of view," Hardo contended.

The headman ignored Hardo's comment. "Forever wandering from one place to the next. Half a year now, with no clothes on your back, and barefoot, a fugitive from the Japanese. No, I don't understand it. I don't understand at all. Everyone is talking about you. Now, praise heaven, at least that has stopped, at least as far as I can tell, anyway. People don't seem to talk about the Rebellion anymore. Maybe even the Japanese have forgotten. And now, when people mention your name, it's whispered softly and in a tone of honor and respect. I'm serious, Hardo." The old man grew more convincing. "The Japanese have forgotten about it. And here, in Kaliwangan, the only people living here are farmers. They're not going to betray you. You can trust me, my son. Sure, we have the watchmen and youth corps just like in other places, but they're a herd of dumb buffalo.

And you know how it is with farmers. They'll believe anything, especially if it's someone educated who's telling them something. They won't betray you. It would be just the opposite. Because they respect you, they'll protect you. So come on home, Hardo. Ramli and his mother are waiting. Your bed hasn't been slept in for ages. And Ningsih replaced the old cover with a new one that's all clean and white. Let's go home!"

"Mmmm . . ."

The old man whispered helplessly to himself, "What am I going to say to Ramli and his mother?" He pulled on his hair like an old woman keening the death of her only son. "Please, Hardo! Have you no care left for me at all? Or for Ramli? Why, he was circumcised just today. Or his mother? When they hear that you refused to come home, what are they going to think? You don't have to stay for long; a little while would do. I still have the buggy. Afterwards, I could take you into the city if that's where you want to go. Try to think about me and how worried I . . ." Left unfinished, his sentence died in the evening air. "Where will you sleep tonight?"

"Mmmm . . ."

"Oh, Heavenly Father, perish the thought that I might someday find you sleeping on the hard ground." He scuffed the dirt with his feet. "Pestered by mosquitoes at night and flies during the day. What would I feel? And if I were to hear that the police had arrested you for loitering, what would people say about me? Wouldn't they blame me? You see, Hardo, everyone thinks of you as my son. Ramli and his mother love you. And Ningsih too. Oh, God the Most Knowing, only He knows what I'm feeling now. Please come home."

The beggar maintained his silence and the starlight that fell upon him showed him picking up clods of earth with his hand. He tossed the clumps of earth just in front of him. For a moment the crickets stopped chirping but a second later began again. From the distance, in the direction of the city, came the creaking sound of a large-wheeled ox cart heading toward Kaliwangan. The chief in his silence and frustration looked exasperated, like a man who had run out of ideas. He took another cigarette from his pocket but then put it back again.

"Ah, that must be my ox cart," the village chief said to lighten the oppressive silence. "This afternoon I had the driver take rice to one of the Chinese dealers to exchange for cigars, some sugar and oil, and a little palm wine. It may be illegal but it might do you some good to share a few shots of the stuff with me. It helps to warm you up." He turned his head in the direction of the sound but the cart, hidden beyond the curve of the road, was not yet visible. "Do you like palm wine?"

"Mmmm . . ."

"Oh, what am I supposed to say? Come home. Please."

Saying nothing, the beggar pulled himself erect, stepped to the center of the road and began to walk slowly in the direction of the city. At once the chief stood too and began to follow him on his left side. He took the beggar's hand and tugged it gently.

"Come home," he said.

"Let go of my hand," the beggar ordered.

The old man dropped the beggar's hand. "Don't you have any feelings at all for Ramli or his mother? Ramli was circumcised today."

"Tell them to wait," the beggar said then.

"To wait?" the village chief repeated hopelessly. "Until when?"

"Until the Japanese have been defeated."

The village chief looked shocked. "Until the Japanese have been defeated? When will that be? The Jap-

anese, defeated? Is that possible? It sounds so strange to
say it . . . the Japanese defeated. You yourself know how
strong their army is. You were an officer once and know
more about it than me. Can the Japanese be defeated?"
He seemed confused.

"The Allied Forces are close. They've landed in
Borneo and will soon be in Java." He stopped speaking
and the two men continued to walk abreast, moving
slowly forward. The beggar began to speak once more
but the soft tone of his voice made his words seem like a
prayer. "A person can't always win. Man lives for victory and then defeat or the other way around."

"I think I'm still a good judge of your character,
Hardo," the old man pronounced, then asked cautiously,
"To win and to lose. Do you have any idea when the
Japanese will be defeated?"

Hardo left the question unanswered and continued
walking slowly down the road toward the city. The wind
whistled as it picked up force. The sky was clear and the
stars flickered safely overhead. The old man kept in step
behind Hardo, his eyes constantly watching Hardo's
back.

"Are you coming with me?" Hardo asked matter-of-
factly.

"Oh God in Heaven," the old man moaned. He
spoke with disappointment. "So, you won't come back
with me?"

In silence the beggar walked forward. The creaking
of the ox-cart wheels grew louder.

"Don't you feel sorry at all for the people at home
waiting for you?" The old man coughed and scratched
his backside. "My eyes aren't what they used to be.
Things aren't as clear for me as they once were. And I
can't really see your features all that well."

The two men passed a tamarind tree. With its

boughs creating a cover for both the road and the edge of the rice field, the tree resembled an open umbrella. The crackling of the dry leaves beneath their feet gave a rhythmic sound to their walk. In the distance before them the street lamps of the city glowed beneath a cape of blue. As they followed the bend in the road, the lamps disappeared. The fields to their left and right were planted with watermelons, cucumbers, and pepper plants. On the road in front of them the shape of an ox cart emerged. Its lantern, hanging from the cart's central beam, swung back and forth with its movement.

"No one will turn you in, son. Come with me, please. Please, Hardo, come home." The old man's voice trembled but still the beggar beside him paid no attention. He walked slowly forward. "Why is it? Why is it that you have no concern for me at all?"

The beggar laughed weakly. "Go home," he urged.

"Go home? Alone, without you? What would Ramli's mother have to say to that?" Sadness and hesitancy lined his voice. "You know how difficult it is for me to stand up to Ramli's mother. You've seen it yourself. If I were to arrive home alone, she'd yell at me and accuse me of not looking for you. And there's nothing worse for a man than to have his wife yell at him. Not a thing! You get this sinking feeling inside and you lose sight of what to do. It makes you feel worthless. Come home with me!"

The beggar continued his march toward the city with the old man faithfully beside him. The creaking of the cart grew clearer. The moon, a reddish yellow and no larger than a palm sheath, began to peek over the eastern horizon. The dark blue sky lost some of its color and the stars that hung next to the moon began to fade. A thin patch of clouds moved across the sky. Brushing past the stars, one by one they disappeared, to reemerge when left behind. The night carried to them the song that the ox-cart driver had begun to sing. It was a common song, one from the repertoire of folk opera songs that have been sung for centuries, completely free from the cold and rigid idealism of the present.

"It must be eight o'clock by now," the chief said sadly. "The guests will be arriving." He waited for the man beside him to say something but he heard no reply. He then spoke to the beggar in a half-coaxing voice. "Don't you miss your father?"

"No."

"I'm sure that he'd like to see you. It's been half a year. And half a year spent in fear and worry is a very long time. If you stopped at Kaliwangan, you could visit him. That would be a nice thing for you to do." The old man coughed and cleared his throat. "Maybe you didn't hear about what happened? Your father . . . your father . . ." He waited to see if he had gained his companion's attention but Hardo continued to stare in silence at the stars. The old man spoke more forcefully. "The Japanese fired him."

"That's good."

"What's good about it?"

"It takes away his power to oppress."

"Dear God, but your father is not the kind of leader who would oppress the people."

"But at the very least, he would help to make their oppression easier."

"Heavenly Prince!" the chief exclaimed. He paused, silent for a moment. "Why do you say that?"

"A person who works for an oppressive regime is an oppressor. It doesn't matter in what position," Hardo laughed. "They're all the same."

"So that means that I am an oppressor too?"

The beggar looked at him and snorted. "Yes, it does."

"God the Most Powerful!" he wheezed. "But without a government in control the place would be taken over by brigands."

"You'll find brigands wherever you go. Even where there is a government you find cold-blooded murder too. So, that being the case, what's the use of a government? Which is better, for a society to have a lot of small thieves or for the government to be a big one? And you too, you are a thief!"

The headman's voice betrayed his surprise. "But in times like these, if there weren't any government, there would be even more problems."

"Rubbish! More problems? The only problem you'd have is that you'd be without an income." Hardo laughed in disdain. "Now go home."

The village chief sighed, then slowly inhaled. In front of the two men, the outline of the cart grew larger. The lantern swung rhythmically, one moment throwing its light forward, the next moment to the back, alternately revealing the left- and right-hand wheels of the cart and the rump of the ox that pulled it. The spokes of the wheels rose and fell, turning slowly and perpetually around.

"I wonder what your father would say if he heard you talking like that?" The headman immediately altered his tack. "Did you hear about your mother?"

"What about her?"

"From Allah we come and to Allah we shall return," the old man mumbled. "Your mother has returned to the lap of our Maker. I pray that heavenly light always shines on her grave." The beggar seemed unmoved by such powerful news. "I don't know what to say," the old man muttered. "It seems useless to even try. You won't talk to me anymore, not like you used to. And you look like a wandering priest who has left this earthly world behind. The life of a wanderer! Well, I pray that you're happy and free from misery and worry. You've given up all your favorite things! Even cigarettes! Your mother and your father! Even my family has no special place in your heart anymore. No, Hardo, I don't understand and cannot imagine what your feelings toward Ningsih must be."

The old man paused as if to recover from the shock of this realization.

"Where is Ningsih?" Hardo asked again, ignoring the man's comments.

"She's in the city!"

"Where?"

"With her friend, a teacher at the Kartini School."

"But Blora doesn't have a Kartini School."

"Really, she's with a Kartini teacher."

The beggar laughed and glanced at the sky. "The star is out again," he said slowly.

"What star?" the old man asked. "What star?" he repeated.

"There, in the sky."

"Where?"

"There, in the sky, and in my heart."

"Your heart?" The old man shook his head. "I don't understand."

"Go home."

"Go home? But if I go home, I should at least take some news about you, And what are you going to do? Are you going to your father's?"

"No."

"Or to visit your mother's grave?"

"No."

"Tell me where you're going."

"To the stars," the beggar answered shortly.

"The star in the sky and in your heart?" the old man muttered in frustration.

"That's right."

"I don't understand at all."

"Go home!"

The chief said nothing. Yellow and shining, the moon in the east was now the breadth of a sword and the shape of a sickle. The ox cart on the road ahead grew larger. Its lantern, a yellow light the hue of the moon, swung incessantly to and fro. The cart driver continued his song. His voice was shrill and far from beautiful but he sang safely, calmly, and happily, as if the prewar days had returned. The ox lifted its legs lazily and moved slowly forward, its rump and tail swaying like a tired pendulum.

"Go home," Hardo said again. "I can't accept your offer. Give my regards your wife, Ramli, and Ningsih. And tell them that I will come to see them."

"When?"

"I've already told you."

"After the Japanese are defeated?"

"Yes."

Silence stood between them. The moon grew larger. The creaking of the ox cart heightened. The chief placed his hand on Hardo's shoulder and held on tightly as if wanting to arrest his movement, but finally, unsure of what to do next, he eased his hold. "That's my cart," he whispered. "We can go back on the cart!"

"Don't touch me again. Go home."

"But what am I going to say?"

"Are you really that afraid of your wife?"

"Yes."

"Tell her that I will return."

"And now where are you going, Hardo? Please tell me."

"To the stars."

"Oh . . ." The old man seemed at once sad and irritated. "How's anyone going to know what that means?"

"That's not my concern; that's their problem," Hardo said quickly as if afraid of being overheard.

"Take pity on Ningsih," the old man said sadly.

"Why should I pity her?"

"Well, if she were to find you in the condition you're in. . . . Come home to the village. I'll ask Ningsih to come. That's it. I'll call her home tomorrow night. No one would ever know. But if she were to see you in this state, she'd surely be upset."

"Upset?"

"Well of course. Women judge things by appearances. The eyes! They place more importance on the eyes than the brain or the heart." He stopped to swallow. "Do you understand?"

"Is that what you think about your own daughter?"

"She's a woman, Hardo. A woman," the headman reminded him. "You have to keep that in mind."

"Then you don't even know your own daughter," he said with certainty.

With the cart approaching, the village chief quickly continued. "You have to keep things in focus, Hardo. Come back. I'll call Ningsih home tomorrow. I'll go get her myself. Please, Hardo, come home!"

"No thank you."

"In fact, I could summon her tonight. How about that? Won't you come home."

"No thanks."

"Heavenly Prince! Only You know how much I want to bring home my son," he prayed slowly "and Ningsih."

The beggar demanded once more, "Where is Ningsih?"

The old man refused to answer. He muttered incoherently and clenched his fists as if ready to fight but then forced himself to be calm. "In the city," he stammered. "She's been there ever since the Japanese started looking for you. But the Japanese have never gone to her place. That's what Karmin said. Karmin makes sure that she's safe. Half a year now it's been. But you don't have to worry. And Ningsih herself said to me, 'I won't come back to the village until Hardo returns.' It's been half a year, and that's not a short time. Won't you come home?"

"Where in the city?" Hardo pressed.

"With her friend from the Kartini School." The village chief was exasperated. "It's late. The guests must be there. Come home!" The tense silence between the men returned. The creaking ox cart came near. "You really won't come home?"

"No," Hardo answered firmly.

"Would you like something to wear?"

"No."

The old man exhaled as he searched his trousers pocket. "There it is," he finally said. "You're lucky I brought some money along. Here's five hundred! Won't you take it?" In his hand was a thin pile of hundred notes. The beggar turned his head slightly back and to the right in the direction of the rice field. "No? You don't want my money either? Don't worry; it won't put me out. I've been selling teak on the black market and the profits are high. If they weren't I wouldn't be able to pay for two days of shadow plays to celebrate Ramli's circumcision. Take it!"

Hardo stared at the cart. "Give it to someone who needs it."

"Everyone needs money."

"Then you use it."

"My God, my God! I don't understand. I don't understand at all." He pocketed the money again.

The crescent moon rose from the horizon. Only fifty meters remained between the two men and the cart. The light of the stars waned and as the wind slackened the clusters of bamboo that flanked the city's edge grew in height. The hollow between the clumps of bamboo appeared to be a gateway leading to the city beyond.

"The cart's almost here," the old man said. "Let's go home," he said to his silent partner. The men listened to the song of the driver as it floated in the calm air. "You really won't come?"

"No," the beggar repeated, annoyed.

"And you don't want the money?"

"No," the beggar responded weakly.

The cart grew closer.

"Where will you go?" The old man's voice was nervous.

"The stars."

"I pray that God watches over you and keeps you safe always," the chief said with a resigned sigh.

"Thank you."

Almost atop them, the driver of the cart called out, "Hey, sir! Hello! Where are you going this time of night?"

"Stop! I'll catch a ride home," the village chief answered. The wheels of the cart were as high as the two men's shoulders. The cart's lantern lit the ground below it, the wheels and the ox's legs and rump, the beam of the heavy cart and the edges of the road. "Well, Hardo. How about it?" the old man said softly.

"Go home."

The cart creaked to a stop. The old man boarded from the back and moved forward to the front.

"The money?"

"Go home." Hardo walked on without turning.

From high on the cart, the driver spoke slowly. "Who was that?"

"Just a beggar." The old man shook his head. "I don't understand it at all."

The two men were again on their separate paths. The beggar walked listlessly forward, but after the cart was at a distance, he turned quickly to the right and entered a narrow path that led through the rice field. He picked up his step and the world around him became completely still. He deftly hopped from one dike to the next. Picking up speed again, he bounded away toward the southeast.

TWO

The moon hung at a forty-five-degree angle and as the night progressed the air cooled. In the distance the bell in the district office building rang faintly, ten times. It was ten o'clock, ten o'clock exactly.

In the moonlight the bamboo fence made of tightly woven staves was a glimmering yellow. Beneath the fence and along its edge, weeds and grass, deep green in color, flourished, and in the moonlight the deep green of the grass appeared even darker. The fence wound along the edge of a rice field, bordering a dike that doubled as a footpath. The gate in the fence, also made of staves, was held closed by a twist fashioned from a tassel of bamboo. Behind the fence was a small field of corn, and with the passing of the night wind the stalks rustled and waved. As the wind died, the plants shuddered and then fell still, as if asleep, like young men shaken and silenced by dream's desires.

The path inside the gate was bordered on both sides by rows of corn. About twenty meters down the path was a hut made of dark palm fronds that had been woven and braided together. The grass that grew on the path lay helplessly flattened, parted by footsteps. At the end of the path the door to the hut yawned open, a deep black hole.

The moon rose higher. The bell in the district office pealed once and a moment later the figure of a man appeared, walking along the dike of the rice field. At the gate in the fence the man stopped. He wore almost nothing. His shoulder blades protruded and the nape of his neck was covered by long hair. The man's skeletal fingers undid the bamboo twist and opened the gate. He stepped inside and closed the gate but did not refasten the loop. He moved slowly toward the hut.

The man wore nothing but a dirty and yellowed loincloth that completely exposed his shrunken thighs. Only his genitals remained hidden. He was the image of a man at odds with an age he could not fit into.

The corn plants that bordered the right and left sides of the path he now traced had changed. He scanned the plants, admiring their size, and noted that it was nearly time to trim and dry the tassels. He stared approvingly at the sheen of the moonlight that clung to the green leaves.

"A good crop of corn," he said to himself as he advanced toward the hut. "But when it is ready to be harvested, the Japanese will come and take two thirds of it." His thin legs trembled. Knobby at their joints, they seemed no bigger than stems of knotty rattan. As he neared the gaping entrance to the hut he spoke to himself again. "But farmers would never make trouble." He went inside.

The hut was dark and the moonlight that enveloped the world outside shone through the holes in the fabric of woven coconut fronds as stars in a darkened sky. The earthen floor of the hut was covered with plaited sheaths of bamboo, on top of which was a woven grass mat.

"He still complains as much as he used to," the beggar said in apparent reference to the village chief. "He hasn't changed a bit. The older he gets the worse he is." The beggar smiled as he lowered himself carefully to a sitting position and leaned back against the upright pole of the hut to watch the path. "All he would say to my questions about Ningsih was 'The city! The city! With her friend at the Kartini school.' That's all he would say." He smiled as he relaxed and lowered his body further, but his eyes remained fixed on the path and the gate in the fence. The night wind made him shiver. "It's so cold," he mumbled.

The coconut-frond roof, secured only by bamboo ties at one end, flapped in the wind. He listened carefully to the chatter of the disturbed fronds, then curled his body into a ball. Looking upward, he could see the pale sky through the holes of the dancing roof. In the sky pallid stars flickered weakly.

"But in the condition I'm in," he asked himself, "who would accept me?" He scratched his head and whispered the name Karmin as if it were the name of a person he had just met. He let out a slight groan and then fell silent, but his mind continued the solitary conversation. "I want to talk with you, Karmin. How long has it been now since we've spoken in a normal fashion! Karmin, you once said that you would join me. Where is your willingness now? No, I don't blame you. But I want to see proof of your will. You are the best commander in the battalion. You know how to handle your men." Suddenly his mind was in turmoil. "Your father is afraid that I'll look for you, Ningsih. So I'm the kind of man they're looking for? I'm the kind of man the government hates?" His inner voice took on new strength. "So be it, then." The voice grew more determined and hard. "In the end, Karmin, you and your platoon will fall into my hands." He took a breath and straightened his curled body.

He was about to open his mouth to express his feelings but the sound of tramping feet stopped him. Outside the hut, he could hear men running on the dike. The slapping and tramping sounds were of bare feet and hard rubber soles. As he listened the sounds became more intense. He heard the ripping sound of a shirt snagged by the fence and then a boisterous cry. "To the east! There! The son of a bitch! Don't let him get away!" His eyes narrowed. As if he himself were preparing to run, his hands and feet clutched the ground. The sound of footsteps grew clearer, the pounding more resonant. He stared at the entrance to the hut.

"Are they after me again?" he asked himself slowly. His body shook. "The Japanese police. . . . Why they're a herd of buffalo at best, only good for eating grass!" His voice weakened. "Why do you have to give me such trouble?"

He heard an order: "If you catch him beat him up!" And then a puzzled cry: "Where the hell did he go?" For an instant the pounding and cries stopped, completely disappeared. He pricked up his ears to hear the cries continue. "That sod of a gambler! Kick him if you catch him." To which was added, "We'll beat the shit out of him!" and "He must have gone to the south."

He heard the sound of footsteps again and saw a dark

and wildly frantic figure, a man, stop before the gate. Quickly but carefully the man opened the gate, closed it again, crouched down, and began to advance toward the hut. The beggar scrambled to the side of the entrance and prepared to run. The shadow of the stooped figure appeared in the doorway. The beggar heard a mumbled complaint. "So this is what I've come to." As the man stepped into the hut the plaited bamboo floor creaked beneath his weight. In the center of the room he stopped and, still breathing hard, sat down and turned to keep his eye on the gate. "What the—!" he cried in surprise when he saw the black shadow beside the door. "Is that a man?" he whispered in fear as he tried to stand.

"Yes, it is," came the short but friendly reply.

The man sighed with relief and sat down again. He was still trying to catch his breath.

The sound of footsteps from the search party outside grew more faint, yet their cries and threats still traveled through the evening air. The older man who had just entered the hut sat where the beggar had been sitting and leaned against the wall support. "No one comes into my place without my permission," he grumbled in displeasure, even as he tried to control his breathing. "Where are you from?" he demanded of the darkened shape.

"Nowhere in particular."

The newly arrived man shifted his body closer to the beggar. "I know that voice," he remarked. "It sounds like . . . it sounds like my son's. Where are you from?"

"Nowhere."

"What do you mean? Are you a traveler or something?"

"That's right," the beggar answered as he turned slightly to face his questioner. He then leaned against the doorpost and pulled his legs up beneath his chin.

"That's not exactly a good thing to be doing in times like these! I feel sorry for you," the man said before resuming his investigation. "Have you been around the Blora area much?"

"I've seen almost all of it."

"All of it?"

"Yes, the whole area."

"And how long have you been doing this?"

"For some time now."

"Your voice is so familiar. It's like my son's."

The beggar laughed weakly. "What's so funny about that?" the man inquired.

The beggar laughed again, then asked the man, "How old are you?"

"Forty."

"I suspect that your hearing is going."

"Could be. Yes, it could be at that. But no, I'm sure of it. My boy's voice sounds just like yours." He stopped speaking as he caught his breath. His chest had stopped heaving. "The watchmen sure are busy these days," he started to explain. "They're always ready to beat up someone. Me for one!" His voice wavered. "And they just about got me too."

"Are you nervous?" the beggar asked.

"No, no, it's not that," the man said, trying to cover his fright. His voice took on a false levity. "Um, well if you really have been all around the area, you might have some good news for me."

"Who are the watchmen looking for?" the beggar inquired, ignoring the conversational lead.

"Me, I guess."

"Why? Are you a thief?" the beggar asked.

"No."

"A rebel?"

"No."

"A gambler?"

"You guessed it," the man sighed. "Yes, I'm a gambler. I was playing with three guys earlier and . . . and you know, we must have a surplus of spies around here. Not you though. Even though I don't know you, I suspect you're not that kind of man. In my life I've come across lots of men like you and all of them have been very open-minded. And you seem even more so!"

"Why's that?"

"Because your voice is just like my son's."

"So?"

"So I trust you, that's why." The man addressed his next comment to himself. "How people can stoop to such a thing just to get by, I'll never understand." The beggar chuckled and the man looked at him in surprise. "It really is, it really is . . . even your laugh is like my son's."

"But I don't have a family," the beggar said in monotone as if reciting a text by rote.

The sound of footsteps forced the old man into silence. The two men listened silently, their eyes on the fence gate. Outside the gate several men passed, walking slowly. A moment later they disappeared from view.

The owner of the hut turned to the beggar once more. "So what are you doing here? What do you have to say for yourself?"

The beggar failed to answer the question. "Are you a gambler?" he asked lightly.

"Yes, I am," the older man murmured. "I never thought I would be, but yes, I am. I just don't care about anything else. I live for cards and the roulette wheel. Ah, there's nothing like it if you have electric lights and maybe a little music on the radio. You know, I could gamble for three days straight and not leave my place. I suppose you don't know . . . I suppose you've never—"

"What don't I know?" the beggar interrupted.

"You don't know what it is that I find in gambling."

"Freedom?" the beggar guessed.

"Exactly. It's freedom! Have you ever gambled?"

"No," the beggar answered. "Except with my life."

"I like that answer. And it's true, I suppose. A guy like you who lives off the road is always gambling with life, anywhere and everywhere he is. But me, I get my excitement at the gaming table. When I'm in front of it, you don't know how happy that makes me."

"You're sick," the beggar accused.

"I am not. I'm in fine health," the older man replied as he slid his backside closer to the wall and straightened his body.

"Yes you are," the beggar reaffirmed as he shifted his body to match the position of the older man.

"I am not," the owner of the hut said in self-defense. "I might have been hurt. I might have had my share of pain and suffering but no, I'm not sick."

"Suffering? What have you suffered?"

"You don't know the half of it," the man said under his breath. "I have suffered a great deal and for a great many things and suspect that anyone else who had gone through what I've had to go through would be crazy by now. I've seen people go mad from pain and suffering. Maybe what you said before is true. I like frankness, my friend! I used to be different. For the people around me I was like a haunted house, frightening to approach and full of deep and dark secrets. That's because I used to be a district chief, you see, not much more than a spy. But not now. I don't have that job anymore and I don't have a bag of secrets to carry around. I like being open. Maybe what you said is true. Maybe I am sick. Ever since I started to gamble, I haven't felt that there's anything real in my life. That even life is just some trick that Nature is playing. Yes, just one of God's games. Especially with the Japanese watchdogs always after me. That's what it feels like—that life is just a game. But you know, they haven't caught me yet. And I've been gambling for months now. Little by little, the gaming table has eaten everything I once owned. But what the hell. Life is just a game. Life isn't real. I don't care if I lose everything. I don't care at all because I have this hunch that life is just a mass of clouds floating across the sky with no one knowing where it's going. And it doesn't matter, just so long as I . . ." He paused to tap his index finger on the side of his forehead. ". . . Just so long as I don't start thinking."

The beggar laughed. "And when you think, what do you think about?" He seemed skeptical.

Keeping his eyes on the gate, the gambler spoke sadly. "My wife, my boy, even me and my job . . ."

As he paused, the wind increased and the ceiling above them began to flutter restlessly. The hut's walls trembled at the wind's insistence. The gambler rested his elbows on his knees and his face in his hands.

"What about your wife?" the beggar asked.

"She's dead," the gambler said sadly. "Five months ago, exactly. And when she died, she took with her my final hold on life. The last one I had. Just look at me, my friend. I have nothing to hold on to anymore. So I can do as I please, whatever I want. I'm like a seed pod. The hull grows harder and harder and in the dry season, suddenly bursts open to eject its pollen, leaving behind an empty shell. After my wife died, my house, my home turned into a jail for me. And I don't like jails. Maybe if you'd gone through what I've gone through, you'd be even worse. But you see, I'm not so crazy. I began to go out at night, and then in the afternoon too, anywhere at all, just so that I didn't have to stay at home. I'd go off with no destination in mind." He drew in a long deep breath.

When he exhaled, his chest rattled. He continued in a low voice, "What you said might be true. Maybe I am sick."

"How did your wife die?" the beggar asked softly.

"How? You sound like a man who doesn't think that death is entirely a matter of God's will. And because of that, I'll answer you. She died from fear." He raised his head to look at the gate again.

"It must have been the Japanese she was afraid of," the beggar said, half guessing.

The gambler looked at him in surprise. "What did you say? You have the guts to say something like that in a time of war?" The excitement in his voice faded. Speaking in a lower tone, he seemed to be talking to himself. "What does it matter? Everyone knows anyway. And I . . ."

The beggar offered no sympathy. "And your son?"

"My son . . ." The gambler hid his face behind his crossed arms and spoke wistfully. "He's the reason for all of this."

The beggar released his hold on his knees. They snapped to the floor with a thud as they hit the bamboo cover. He groped for the door frame with his left hand and then stretched out his legs.

"My son used to be an officer, a platoon leader in the Indonesian Volunteer Army. Oh, I knew about his real feelings toward the Japanese," the gambler explained. "I knew for some time what he was feeling inside. And I think I knew that the day was going to come when he couldn't keep his feelings inside any longer. And that made me afraid. I was so afraid." He paused as if remembering something. "He'd come home on leave from the Cepu barracks, and whenever he came I could see how dissatisfied he was with the Japanese. As time went by, his feelings became all the more apparent. And I told him once, 'You're still young, but think of your parents.'

That's all I told him. What else could I say? But he never said anything."

The old man lifted his head and stared at the beggar. "Did you hear what I said?"

"Yes, yes, go on."

The gambler rested his head in his hands again. "Your voice is like my boy's." He sat silently, drunk with confusion, then continued in a low voice, "I guess he never heard my advice. He certainly didn't follow it. One time he came home to tell me, 'Father, I've come to say good-bye,' and then he left. And then afterwards . . ." The man's chest rose as if he were trying to catch his breath.

"You're a good father," the beggar said, consoling the gambler.

The man said nothing to this. The oppression of the night enveloped them. The gambler leaned toward the door, looked momentarily at the gate, then sat upright again. He heaved a heavy sigh. "Maybe I am," he said wearily, "but I've never really thought about whether I was a good father or not. I never thought about myself as a father, much less a good one. Maybe I am." The night's stillness bore down upon them once more.

The beggar spoke carefully. "But there's no real need for you to be sad."

The old gambler's legs and torso twisted as he shook his head. "Sad? It's not really sadness that I'm feeling. It's just that I've lost my hold on things. Yes, I've lost my hold. I don't know anymore what I'm supposed to do or who to work for. And given the condition I'm in it's difficult to see what kind of future awaits me. But no, I'm not sad. I just feel that life is empty. Empty, empty, completely empty!"

"Empty? I too have felt emptiness. And I know how unsettling and frightening that can be. But what about your son?" the beggar said in commiseration. "What happened then?"

"Well, then . . ." The gambler stopped, unsure. "Then," he continued slowly, "the news came. . . ." He paused again and leaned his head back until it touched the wall behind him. In that position his eyes searched the ceiling.

"What news?" the beggar asked, covering the gap in conversation.

The gambler's head fell suddenly forward; his eyes locked on his guest. "Your voice is just like my son's!" The beggar laughed. "But no . . ." The gambler denied such hope. "My boy has to be dead. The Japanese aren't famous for forgiving their enemies. And that network of spies they have is very tight. If he could escape that . . ."

"But what was the news?" The beggar ignored the man's theories.

"The news was that my son had been involved in a rebellion against the Japanese army, that three commanders had led their platoons in revolt. You heard about it, didn't you?" The gambler's voice contained a hint of pride.

"I did hear something. I suppose all of Java has," the beggar added lightly. "But if I heard right, the rebellion was a failure."

"Yes, it was," the gambler quickly affirmed before hiding his face in his arms once more. "Word is that one of the leaders betrayed the others. I wonder if you can feel, if you have any idea what a parent feels to have his child on the run, especially when who's looking for him is the Japanese military government. They'd as soon kill you as look at you. You must have some notion of what I feel. After that I, his own father, received a telegram, an order from the government to mobilize a search party for my son. Imagine! Can you think of anything worse? For a father to have to hunt down his own son and to turn him over to his executioners? Think of it! The telegram I received added that my son had fled to Blora." The gambler paused to emit a deep groan, then continued in a low, hoarse voice. "Only God knows how glad I was when my boy wasn't found; when he escaped from the cordon of people and military patrols." His voice slowed. "But that wasn't the end of it. I got another telegram, this one saying that my boy had been seen in the Plantungan Mountains. I was ordered to mobilize the people again."

The beggar joined the old man in taking a deep breath. He scratched his shoulders and the sound it produced was that of dry corn leaves rubbing together.

"The women too?" the beggar inquired. The gambler said nothing. "Your wife was ordered to go along too?"

"Oh, dear God!" the gambler cried. "Yes, they made my wife go too. How such a thing could be happening I found it nearly impossible to comprehend. How could God let this happen? It wouldn't have been so bad if she had been in good health. But after learning that our boy was a fugitive from the Japanese, she had taken ill. And when the order came, when the order came to go after him, her health deteriorated. But she was made to go and was delirious most of the way. 'My son, my son!' she kept moaning. You must have heard about it: four thousand people mobilized to trap my son! Only God knows how thankful I am that he wasn't caught. But . . ." His voice quavered. "But for my son's life we had to pay with my wife's." The beggar sighed. "Two hours after returning home, she died." Silence hung in the air. The old man slowly raised his head, uncrossed his arms, and lay down.

Having lost the gambler's attention, the beggar too lay down, his body parallel to that of the other man.

There was tension in the air. Both men seemed to be afraid to speak, to chase away the shadows that now darkened their thoughts. The night wind whispered in the frond roof and whistled as it slipped through the holes in the walls. The rustling of the dry corn leaves intensified the tension inside.

Slowly and as if frightened the beggar finally spoke. "What happened to your son?"

"Ah, if only someone knew." The gambler's lips scarcely moved as he uttered this. "Oh, my boy . . . it's been so long. Maybe the Japanese have cut off your head. That's what they would do. They might not say much but they act, and killing for them is just a matter of course. But no one knows what happened to him or where he went. For him, that's good. And you know, after those first two telegrams, I got a third one, this one telling me that I was no longer needed to find my boy because . . . because I had been relieved of my position."

"What was that?"

"District head. I am the former district head of Karangjati," the former official said proudly. "If you've been around these parts for a while, you should know that the city of Blora was under my jurisdiction."

"A district head, huh? But what kind of district head sleeps with a beggar in a hut?"

The gambler turned toward the beggar with open eyes. Like a man trying to climb an embankment, he raised himself to look down at his companion on the floor. "And what kind of beggar are you?" he frowned before reclining again. "Well, so be it," he said despondently. "So what if this former district head has a beggar sleeping beside him? That's right, I keep forgetting. No wonder you smell so bad." He mused silently. "But are you really a beggar?" Skepticism flooded his voice.

The beggar gave a short laugh but said nothing.

From the direction of the road off to the north came the revving of an automobile. Once, twice, three times.

"What's an automobile doing out on the road at this time of night?" The beggar seemed puzzled. "What time is it now?"

"Around eleven."

"Eleven o'clock and there's an auto on the road. But listen, that sounds more like a truck than a car."

"A truck, that's it!" the gambler confirmed.

"Probably troops from Cepu."

"Probably." The former district head looked the beggar over with detachment. "Hey, if you really are a beggar, how come you're so smart."

"Smart?" The beggar seemed disinterested.

"That's right. Beggars don't talk about such things. If you're a beggar you should be telling me about the dead chicken you found and the meal you made of it." The beggar laughed. "And here you are, talking about trucks and cars and what they sound like. . . ." He paused for a moment. "It used to be I liked it when an automobile came to the district residence. That used to make me happy. I liked to receive Japanese guests. I'm sure you can guess why: the thought of a raise or the possibility of a better position! And I'm sure you know that because you're not really a beggar. A civil servant, my friend, has two hopes only: one, better money, and two, a better position. You know that. But now, the sound of automobiles frightens me. I'm always afraid. I have this never-ending fear and I don't know why."

"Especially when you're gambling," the beggar said. "Is that right?"

"That's right," the gambler and former district officer affirmed. "Because if they catch you gambling," he explained, "they make you eat all the money on the table and then they beat you till you're black and blue."

The beggar's chuckle mocked the old man. "What that means then is that the combination of what happened to your wife, your son, and your position turned you into a gambler?" As the old man said nothing the beggar softened his voice. "Because of your wife's death, your son's rebellion against the Japanese, your dismissal as district head, and your own disturbing thoughts . . ."

"Yes, yes." The gambler agreed quickly enough to prevent the beggar from continuing. He spoke dispiritedly. "That's what made me what I am now. All the thoughts I had running around in my head got to be such a burden." He crawled across the floor to lean against the bamboo support. "Think of it. Me, sitting alone in my room with nothing to do and no one to talk to. Having only the specter of the military police chasing me. I'd see the shining sword circling above my head and shudder and start to scream. And I wouldn't snap out of it until my neighbors came running into the house and barged into my room. Only then would I realize that nothing had happened to me, that there was no executioner and no sword; that there was only myself, alone and afraid. In times like that all I could do was curse myself and try to pull myself together enough to convince my neighbors to go away." He hugged his knees together and propped his head on top of them. "Finally, I came to the conclusion that I was going crazy." He suddenly chortled. "At night when all there is are lamps to signal that there is still life in this world, and when all around me is silence, I look in the darkened corners of my room and I can see the face of my boy, thin and haggard, kneeling on the ground, his eyes covered with a band of white cloth. Behind him stands a big, muscular Japanese executioner swinging his sword. And I close my eyes, hide my face in the pillow, and cover my ears with my hands."

"You're sick," the beggar concluded once more.

"Yes, I'll admit it now; at that time I was a bit un-stuck. I knew that but if you really are a beggar you wouldn't be talking about the state of my health, especially my mental health." He waited for the beggar to respond and received not an answer but silence. "But who cares whether you're a beggar or not? When I turn out the lights I see my wife's eyes, just her eyes, watching my every movement. All I can do is whisper, 'Go away! Go away!' And when her eyes have finally closed, her lips appear. And they move as if to say to me . . ." He lifted his head to look at the beggar, who had been drawn closer to him, like a needle to a magnet.

"What do they say?" The beggar sat and stared at the gambler, the former district head. For some time the two men looked into each other's eyes. The beggar urged the gambler to continue. "And then?"

The gambler slowly leaned closer to the beggar and whispered, "Maybe you are my boy." His voice rose in a blend of hope and pain. "Are you my boy?" He silently held his breath.

"You're sick!" came the accusation once more. The beggar now distanced himself slightly from the other man.

"Maybe I am," the gambler agreed before retreating to where he had been sitting. He hugged his knees again and once more rested his head on them.

"What does your wife say?" the beggar asked carefully.

Now the gambler was suspicious and raised his head from his knees. "What's it to you anyway?"

The beggar exhaled. "One thing I know is that people like to share their suffering with others, with the whole world for that matter. This is a cursed age we're living in. You know that too. And the worst thing about it is that you can't talk about your problems with others.

But I understand. So now you have me; you have someone to talk to. Look at me. I'm a traveler, an itinerant
beggar. And beggars are not as greedy as people might
think." He watched the gambler in his desperate confusion. The old man sighed. "Why do you sound so
sad?"

The gambler shook his head. The night hung in silence around them.

"You're still suspicious of me." The old man still
said nothing. "There's no reason for me to lie. Yet you're
still suspicious of me."

"No, I'm not. But your voice is just like my son's."
The gambler's voice trembled. "If only you were my
son . . ." He hid his face in the crook of his arms and
paused to catch his breath.

"I want to know what your wife said," the beggar
told the gambler.

"She'd say," the gambler continued, "she'd say, it's
our boy that's causing me this pain."

"Oh, my God . . ." The beggar sighed. "She was in
pain because of her son."

"Yes, I suppose so," the gambler said sadly. "Tell
me," he asked, "can you imagine anything worse? And
that's the position I was in. Fortunately, I finally got
enough of my senses together to conclude that I was
going to get even worse if I didn't find a way to release
some of my feelings. And so, for the first time in my life,
I began to go out at night—in no certain direction and
always by myself. I forced myself to go out. God, I remember the full moon! I went on foot to Plantungan, the
ridge of limestone hills between the Tempuran reservoir
and Pamotan. I heard rumors that my son was there. And
so I went there to find him. I had to find him. That's the
only thing I could think about." He spoke more slowly.
"If you've been wandering about the Blora area, you

must know the area around Plantungan and the reservoir. Have you been to Tempuran?"

"Yes, it's a beautiful place."

"Extraordinary."

"Very much so."

The gambler spoke lightly. "And now we have a beggar who appreciates beauty too! The Plantungan hills are lovely too, aren't they?"

As if trying to remember something, the beggar remained silent. "Plantungan?" he asked in a monotone.

"Yes, that's where most of the water for the city comes from."

"That's right. Yes, I was once in Plantungan."

"Tell me, are you really my son?"

"You're sick! That's why you can't keep your thinking straight," the beggar rebuked. "If you can't think straight you have to stop listening to yourself. If your son rebelled against the Japanese, then you shouldn't even hope that he's alive or is going to come back home to you. Give it up! Listen to my advice. No, maybe not. Maybe for you it would be better to go on gambling until you really do go mad." He spoke more lightly. "So you didn't find your son?"

"No. But the people there told me about a cave, Sampur Cave, they call it, but I couldn't find anyone with the nerve to go in it. They said it was a haunt for ghosts and devils. Really. I couldn't find anyone to show me the way inside. I offered them fifty *rupiah* and they thought it was a joke. So I bought a long rope and a torch from one of the people and do you know what I did? I went inside the cave by myself! I tied one end of the rope around a stave that I pounded in the ground at the entrance to the cave and I tied the other end around my waist. In one hand I carried the twist of rope and in the other my torch. I went inside but didn't find my son.

The only thing I found was thousands of bats that darted around and kept diving at the flame of my torch. The bodies of the bats that struck the flame rained down on my arm. Inside the cave I found a hot spring spurting out of the center of a rock." The gambler suddenly changed the topic of conversation to ask, "Are you hungry?"

"No," the beggar answered shortly.

"If you are, we can grill ourselves some corn. There's nothing better than hot corn on a cold night. Working in that field out there is what I do during the day. I gamble at night. I left my house and everything in it in the city. Little by little I've sold my belongings for food and gambling money. What do you like to eat?"

"What kind of question is that? Man lives because of food. Without it, he dies."

"I see you have your own opinions on that too. For a beggar you're strange. I can't imagine a real beggar saying something like that." The gambler's voice wavered as he continued. "Maybe everyone thinks that but no one ever says it. Anyway, in the morning after my failed attempt to find my son, I returned home by foot." His voice changed. "If I'm not mistaken, that's about fifteen kilometers and probably the farthest I've ever gone on foot. Outside of Blora I came across a group of boys who were tending cattle and buffalo. To relieve the boredom of watching their herd, they were gambling with tamarind seeds. God, there was such a look of happiness on their faces as they stared at their cards. I sat there a long while watching them. And I came to the conclusion that maybe, if I were to gamble, I too could free myself from the things that were disturbing my mind."

"And so you started to gamble?"

"And so I started to gamble. Yes, because in gambling I find complete freedom. Freedom from the workings of my mind and the memories of my wife and my son."

The beggar laughed sharply. "Great. You won your freedom but in the process you tied yourself with a dead knot to the leg of the gaming table."

"Maybe so. But all I know is that there's no such thing as a free man. You get rid of one bond only to tie yourself to another. Freedom is just a momentary absence of ties, nothing more. What do you think?"

"I think that no one is completely sane, that everyone has his own sickness to deal with."

"What?" The gambler's raised voice sounded angry.

"No one is completely sane."

"You're the crazy one now," the former district head accused. "You're warped," he said slowly. The beggar laughed. "Why are you laughing?" At that the beggar laughed some more. "Because no one is sane? I suppose everyone's crazy but you're not?"

"No, everyone, including myself. If I could find but one sane person in this world, just one . . ."

"What's a beggar talking about that for anyway?" the former district head interjected with a tone of surprise and irritation.

"Don't forget—beggars are human too. Your forgetfulness is just one sign of your mental state. Yes, it's a sign that no one is completely sane." He laughed. "But forget about that. The fact is you're a gambler, a man willing to give up his possessions and his years to free himself from his troubled mind." The gambler sighed. "And to be a slave to the gaming table."

The gambler raised his voice. "You're no beggar! I'm sure of it. You haven't once mentioned dead chickens or poaching ducks in the river. All you can talk about is my gambling. Who are you really?" There was no answer. "Who are you?" Still receiving no answer, the former district chief went on: "I admit it. I am a gambler, a slave of the gaming table. Does that make you happy? And what do I intend to do? Nothing. I have no intention of freeing myself from my bondage."

"You're sick," the beggar said again.

The gambler raised his head to peer at the beggar but found him in almost total darkness. "Why do you keep saying that? Okay, I'm sick, I admit it. But why do you have to keep on saying it?"

"What do you think you'll achieve by throwing away your possessions and your remaining years as a slave?" The tone of the beggar's voice was that of a teacher to a student.

"Me? I'm not trying to achieve anything. Why should I? I don't have a wife or a son or even the friends I used to have. All I have is fear, perpetual fear and a constant desire to gamble. What am I going to achieve? You tell me. And what's the use anyway? I consider it a blessing to be able to free myself from my boredom and anxiety. But you, my friend, what are you trying to achieve by pitting your life against nature?"

"At the very least, a freedom that is greater than the freedom you've found."

"What kind of freedom is that?"

"Freedom from oppression."

"Oppression?"

"Yes, oppression. The oppression of a people who should not be oppressed. Do you understand?" He waited for an answer.

The former district head grumbled, "It's all because of the Japanese that it's like this now. They're proud and demand respect but treat their enemies like animals. Whether they're aware of it or not, they have been digging their own grave. They don't think that Indonesians can see their faults. Well, the Indonesians are most certainly aware of the cruelty of their 'teachers.'" He stopped speaking and was calm again.

Without a sound the moon had risen higher, and in the hut, the darkened hut, the only sound was of two men breathing in unison.

The former district head continued. "You know, if I were still a civil servant, you would be such easy prey for me."

"Well, I'm glad you're a gambler then. The only victim is you—your possessions, your body, and your health. And you're going to keep on gambling until you suck dry whatever pleasure you can find in yourself. I think it's entirely appropriate that you were dismissed from your position. But do you know what's going to happen?"

The gambler seemed confused. "What are you talking about?"

"Someday, I don't know when and I'm sure you don't know either, you'll be found sprawled lifeless on the road with your eyes wide open, staring at the sky."

"Stop!" the gambler insisted.

"But that's what I see."

"Well don't go on," the gambler said with fright. "Who are you really?" His shrill voice was dense with suspicion. "Oh, my God, you're a watchman sent to find me! Or a spy trying to find my son. Tell me! Are you a spy?" He waited in terror for an answer. "Is that what you are?" His fear mounted but the beggar said nothing. "I've lost my wife, my son, my position, my wealth, and myself and now you're going to feed me to the sword?"

The beggar laughed weakly and said coldly, "You're a coward. You're a slave to your gambling. You've traded your life for freedom from a troubled mind. Yet you're afraid of winding up at the end of an officer's sword?"

"I don't know, I just don't know!" the former district officer cried helplessly.

"No," the beggar chided, "I'm not a spy. But I pity you for making your life your stake for the gaming table."

"What you say might be true," said the gambler, not quite believing himself, "but if you're trying to achieve freedom from oppression, and you're trying to do it alone, then you don't know how the world works. The world is full of oppression and suppression. And if in trying to achieve your goal you challenge this system of oppression, do you know what is going to happen? You'll have to face the whole world." The gambler snorted and laughed. "You'll have the whole world to face. The whole world, my friend. And in a matter of seconds, you'll find yourself out of breath." He suddenly seemed more sure of himself. "That's why you're a beggar— because of your dream of trying to change the world." His tone implied victory. "Isn't that right?" The beggar didn't answer. "Yes, that's why you're a beggar." His voice grew more sharp and cynical. "Freedom from oppression? Rubbish! You'll end up a sacrificial lamb, dying in your own entrails."

At this statement the beggar gasped. Afterward, night's calm returned and the two men sat in silence. From far away, somewhere in the southwest, came the repeated sound of a gong. From the north came the sound of vehicles. One, two, three. Three trucks, they supposed, coming from the direction of Cepu and heading toward Rembang.

The beggar finally whispered, "No, the fact is no one is completely sane. And there's no such thing as complete freedom. There's nothing that's one hundred percent in this world. That's just a dream in a dreamer's mind." He began to laugh uproariously and the gambler, the former district head, exhaled a sigh as deep and dark as the night. "All the same," the beggar continued, "we have to try to free ourselves from our present bonds and to climb upward, even if it means that we will be bound again. Freedom is upward, not downward!"

"But I feel like I'm going downward, forever downward," the gambler commented sadly. "And that I'll keep on going down until I reach the very depths of depravity. I'm aware of it. I know what I'm doing, but I feel unable to stop. Maybe in a year or two, after I've used up all my savings and belongings . . ." He sounded bitter. "After I have nothing left as ante for the gambling table."

"You will lie on the road and with fading eyesight gaze upward at the sky, your mouth agape, your breath coming in starts." The gambler began to sob. "And no one will pay you any attention at all. No eyes will take pity on you, even though you once were a district head."

"Oh, dear God," the gambler cried pitifully.

It was silent for a moment as the night wind carried its coolness into the hut. The two men hunched their shoulders.

"And the flies will gather round you," the beggar went on, "and the news will spread that the former district head of Karangjati—uh, what's your name?"

"Mohamad Kasim."

"Everywhere the news will be heard that Mr. Mohamad Kasim, the former district head of Karangjati and petty gambler, died in the middle of the road. And a moment later the people will have completely forgotten the news. Meanwhile, you will have been rolled up in an old mat and thrown into a grave."

The gambler found himself agreeing with the scenario. "But what can I do to free myself?"

"What? When you're dead do you want to be rolled up in an old mat? I would say that is about as low as a person can go. For myself, I might be a beggar but I'm not going to die like that. I'd rather have my head cut off by the Japanese."

"It gives me the chills to hear you say such things," the gambler said in fright. "But maybe there's still a way out." He seemed to be talking in his sleep. "I am of royal blood. My grandfather is buried in the royal cemetery of Imogiri and my father in the royal cemetery of Solo. And I? Am I to be wrapped in a mat and dumped into a grave? In the afterlife what would my ancestors say to that? I am of warrior blood, a descendant of Gatotkaca, who fell in the ancient Bharatayudha War, an offspring of Abimanyu, felled in that same war. Am I to die beside the road, a gambler?" He now spoke directly to the beggar. "There has to be a way out," he consoled himself. "But what is it? What is the antidote? I feel like a beggar sleeping under a bridge and dreaming of a palace! Ridiculous! To even dream about such a thing in these times is mad. It's futile!" The man now seemed confused and melancholy. "If there were a miracle, if my son were to suddenly appear before me, no longer a fugitive of the Japanese . . ."

"You really do love your son."

"He's all I have."

"So if your son were to suddenly appear with the Japanese no longer after him, you'd stop being a gambler?"

"Yes, I think so."

"Is that possible?"

"Why not?"

"I suspect you might stop for a moment but that after he was back for a while, you'd start again."

"No, I wouldn't, I swear."

"But that's a rather slight possibility, isn't it?"

"That I would start gambling again?"

"No," the beggar said forcefully, "that your son would suddenly appear no longer on the run from the Japanese?" His tone lightened. "But who knows, this world is full of miracles. And now, with the Allied Forces so close, the Japanese defenses are falling one by one." He paused. "Oh, and what else was it? You said you looked for your son in Sampur Cave but didn't find him. Who knows, you might find him someday. When you crawled through the cave with the rope tied round your waist and prayed at the spring—"

"What?" the gambler erupted in surprise. "Were you there too?" He turned to face the beggar. His eyes bored into the man in front of him.

The beggar tried to hide his surprise. "I told you that I've been all over."

"But I didn't tell you that I had prayed by the spring," the gambler argued. "You must have been there too! So, maybe you are my son after all," he said slowly, frightened.

"No, I'm not. You're letting your mind run. I'm alone in this world. I told you before not to listen to your confused thoughts," he reminded the gambler. "But as I said, this world is full of miracles. Because, yes, I did see you in that cave. I was there seated on one of the ledges when you called out, 'Hardo! Are you here, Hardo?'"

"Then you must have known who I was."

"You're confused."

"Had you not, you wouldn't have recognized me or my voice or remembered what I said."

"I have a good memory."

Confused once again, the gambler spoke dispiritedly. "I suppose so . . ." But a moment later he regained his hope. "You didn't say anything?"

"No, I didn't."

"Why didn't you say something?"

"Why should I have?" the beggar laughed. "Is Hardo your son?"

"My one and only. I wish you had said something. Why didn't you say anything?"

"I watched you pray five times, but then a bird hit your torch and the fire went out. Isn't that what happened?"

"Yes, it is," the gambler cried with a mixture of surprise and happiness. "Then . . . then did you see my son too in Sampur Cave?" He moved closer to the beggar and whispered excitedly, "If what people said is true, my son had to have been in there too. Did you see him?"

"Every day. I know him well."

"He's alive!" the gambler screamed wildly and threw his arms around the beggar. Without the strength to thwart the man's embrace, the beggar fell backward. The two men rolled together on the floor of the hut. The gambler's voice was hoarse. "You are my son. Stay here. Don't run! You are my son!" His chest heaved as the beggar struggled to free himself. The gambler cried shrilly, "Don't go away!" The bamboo floor creaked as the two men wrestled. The walls rustled as the hut shook. "Don't go!" The gambler's voice weakened. Their legs flailed in the air, while the gambler tried to pin the beggar down and the beggar struggled to get away. The sound of their quickened breathing filled the room. "Don't leave me," the gambler moaned.

"Let me go," the beggar pleaded.

"But you'll run away," the gambler insisted.

"In God's name, I will not run away," the beggar said weakly.

The gambler loosened his embrace, but with his hand held on tightly to the arm of the man he thought to be his son. The two sat together, both weakened by their struggle. Their breathing was swift and hard. The wind caused the roof to flap, and whistled through the walls.

"Please let me go," the beggar said.

"You won't run away, will you?" the frightened gambler asked before standing and moving to the middle of the doorway. He loosened his grip on the beggar, but only slightly.

"For God's sake, I'm not going to run away," the beggar insisted. Finally, the gambler released the beggar's arm and concentrated on controlling his breathing.

"God, you're sick!" the beggar muttered.

"Not this time," the gambler said defensively. "Not this time, I'm not. You are my son, I will swear before God that you're my son. I'm not wrong. I know I'm not. I couldn't be; I knew from the beginning it was your voice."

"You're delirious!"

"No, I'm not. I'm really not."

"You're sick," the beggar said slowly. "I am not your son. But one thing I'm sure of is that you're a good father. And I know that your son loves you very much. But remember"—his voice was sharp—"I am not your son. No, don't interrupt me. Let me have my say. I'll tell you about your son, but don't try to get me to say that I am your son. Do you promise? Will you do that?"

Immersed in his thoughts, the gambler stared at the roof of the hut. He coughed slightly as he whispered nervously to himself, "He really is my son. I'm not sick. I'm as healthy as I was the day I got married."

"Are you going to listen?" the beggar persisted. The

old man beside him ground his teeth in sadness, confusion, and fear. "Listen to me. I know your son. When you came into the Sampur Cave the two of us were sitting on top of a limestone ledge near the peak of the cave. When we saw the light from your torch we ran away. Are you going to listen?" The gambler stared at the roof, and through its cracks at the glimmering sky. "Well, I guess you don't . . ." The beggar waited for the man to say something but the former district head refused to change his stance. The beggar continued regardless in a soft and patient voice. "Your son is alive and well. Believe me. He is still there now. Do you believe me?"

The gambler sighed heavily and mumbled a prayer in Arabic. One moment he was looking out at the gate in the fence, the next moment he was lying on the floor.

"You need not worry about your son. He's alive and well," the beggar continued. "But I warn you! Don't go there again. It would be a waste of time because you will never find him. If you won't listen and insist on going there, you will risk his affection for you. You should know why. He thinks you're still the district head and in that position you are his enemy, no different from the Japanese even though you are his own father. Do you want me to go on? I can stop. Why won't you answer me?"

The beggar paused but the gambler said nothing. Outside the hut, nature's drama continued: the wind, the moon, the sky, plants, animals, and clouds.

"Listen to the sounds," the beggar advised, changing his tack. "Don't listen to what your mind is telling you. You're not well. I know that. Follow my advice. Listen to my voice. I never thought that I would meet the father of my friend Hardo. Would you like to give me a message for him?"

The gambler moved slowly and asked wearily, "Aren't you really my son?"

"How many times do I have to tell you? I'm not your son. Is there anything you want to tell him?"

"Tomorrow morning I'll leave for Plantungan," the gambler said to himself. Motionless, the beggar watched him in silence. "I'll take a couple of bunches of Ambon bananas. Those are his favorite. And I'll go by foot to show him what I would do for his sake. I'll give him proof of what I would do just to see him again."

"It would be better if you didn't go there," the beggar advised. "You'll never find the place."

"But it's been half a year. And what does he have to eat there?"

"Bats."

"Bats!" the gambler shrieked. "The son of a district head eating bats? Are you serious?"

"But you're no longer a district head. You're a gambler."

The former district head coughed in embarrassment. "Yes, I forgot. I'm not a district head. I'm just a petty gambler."

The beggar grunted in amusement. "Why are you surprised to hear that he eats bats when other people have to eat snails and dead chickens?"

"Because he is my son."

"Only because of that?"

The gambler ignored the question. "That's what he's been eating for half a year?"

"For the entire time," the beggar answered coolly. "And with no complaint at all. Or, if he has complained, I have never heard him. And he's as strong as a buffalo." He moved toward the door and stuck his head outside. "It's so clear out tonight." He looked back inside. "Don't go there. What I've told you should be enough news for you. He's safe and well and doesn't need anything from anybody."

"I'm his father and in the morning I'm going to find him."

"But you don't own him. And if you insist on going, I'm telling you, he will not accept you. Believe me!"

The gambler's cry was close to a scream. "Oh, my son. My boy, an ascetic!? I never thought it possible. How could you renounce the world? You are descended from holy men, I know. But where did you find the strength? Look at me. I forget the world through gambling." He spoke as if in a trance. "Your grandfather, he wasn't an ascetic but your great-grandfather was. You are a descendent of Arjuna, the ultimate warrior prince, who gained his powers from meditation. Meditation . . . can you imagine, in this day and age of technology?"

"Technology?" the beggar rejoined. "Hardo once said that meditation is the road that leads directly to one's inner self, and that technology may lead you there as well, but never directly."

The gambler suddenly forgot his sadness. "What are you talking about? You, a beggar, discussing philosophy?" He sat up and squinted his eyes to see his companion better. "A beggar talking about technology and philosophy? Oh, what do I care? What else did he say?"

"That technology can lead man to achievement, that machines provide a source of strength to complement man's own. I once saw Hardo take a light bulb and hold it in his hands. He then asked me 'Do you believe that man holds electricity within him?' And the bulb he was holding suddenly grew bright and then died, its filament broken."

"My son did that?" Mohamad Kasim gasped with pride. "Are you really not my son?"

"No, I'm not!" The beggar seemed angry. "Don't ask me that again." The gambler looked away. His taut body lost its strength and he leaned wearily, acquiescent, against the bamboo pole. "But what's the use of talking about this now," the beggar asked in apology.

"No, that's all right. I want to hear everything you have to say about him. He is my son, after all," the gambler stated humbly.

At this comment the beggar laughed. "Can't you see what you would do by going there? You could lead the Japanese to him! That's why you shouldn't try to find him. He is safe and well. If that's enough for him, that should be enough for you."

The gambler sighed.

"So no more questions. I would like to sleep for a bit. Do you mind?"

"Aren't you hungry?"

"No."

"Why don't you sleep too," the beggar suggested. The mat-covered floor creaked as the beggar lay down. Outside the night was calm.

"My poor boy," the gambler whispered. "Such a long way he has had to travel. Maybe tomorrow I'll be able to talk with him." He stood and stepped carefully outside. The floor moaned weakly beneath his feet.

The night was so peaceful, nature itself seemed dead. The leaves of the corn plants and all other objects were fixed in place, motionless beneath the yellow moon. The gambler stood in the doorway of the hut, a watchman on duty. He stared ahead. A moment later he heard the regular breathing of the beggar.

"That was fast," the gambler whispered. "Asleep already." He walked slowly toward the gate of the fence. Looking up at the moon, he prayed, "May God protect you always."

Nothing disturbed the night's calm. Even the faint sounds of gongs and drums coming from southwest seemed to heighten the sense of calm and the intense stillness that saturated the night air. The rapid but rhythmic sounds were accompaniment for the Flower Battle in the shadow play, in which ogres contest human warriors and inhumanity is faced with humanity. The gongs rising and falling in sure and tempered melody and the disjointed but rhythmic pounding of the drum illustrated the order that can be found in confusion.

Arriving at the gate, the gambler stopped beside it to inspect the dry water channel. Its earthen base was cracked and the cracks appeared a rich black in the moonlight.

The gambler mumbled drowsily as he spoke. "So I'm not supposed to go see my son? Why? I'm his father, am I not? His own father. I'm not supposed to go see him because I'm a former district head?" He turned around and walked slowly back toward the hut. "He's probably asleep." He went in the door. "Are you asleep?" he asked the motionless form. "He's asleep," the gambler confirmed before turning and running back to the gate. "He's asleep. Now's a good time for me to go gambling."

At the gate he stopped suddenly, arrested by his thoughts. "You fool. What am I doing? Maybe he is my son. Why not? He could be. This world is full of miracles. Who knows? Why couldn't he one day wondrously appear before me, no longer a fugitive of the Japanese? He agreed to stay, didn't he? Maybe he is my son. He could be— His arm! Why didn't I think of it before? There should be a scar on his right arm."

He spun around and ran back toward the hut. His hand groped in his pocket for a lighter. A short distance from the doorway he stopped before advancing more slowly toward the dark building. Beside the doorway he listened for the beggar's deep and steady breathing, then slowly entered. The beggar was talking in his sleep. "Karmin, come back," he said.

The gambler knelt to study the beggar more closely. He held the unlit lighter in his hand. Then the beggar mumbled something else. "Ningsih . . . where are you?"

The former district head stood up quickly. He threw the lighter into his sack—he no longer had the nerve to shine it on the beggar's face—and stumbled out of the hut. His eyes searched the sky wildly. "My son!" he whispered ecstatically. "It is my son!" He stared at the moon. "Karmin—I remember. He's the officer who betrayed him. Oh, my boy, you've made so much trouble for so many people. Thousands! But even more for your own parents. And now you've come back to me. Of course, I would . . . of course I'd accept you back. I would accept you as the son you are, just as I once held you when you were born." He covered his mouth with the palm of his hand to stifle his howling cry at the moon. "My son! My son!" His hand dropped limply from his mouth. He then raised his hands to cover his eyes. Finally, he whispered, "And Ningsih, your fiancée . . . no, my son, you can't deceive me. You really are my son."

As if startled by something, he suddenly stamped his foot on the ground. "My son—you are my son," he whispered hoarsely while noticing his field and its rows of corn. "He's probably not eaten." Then he leapt off the path to disappear into the corn patch.

The music of the gongs and drums had disappeared, to be replaced by the rustling of corn leaves and the snapping of stalks. The gambler, the former district head, finally emerged from the patch, his arms cradling a pile of young corn. Moonlight brightened the glow on his face, and the gleam in his eyes was that of a child who has just found a coin. He walked with short quick steps back to the hut. Beside it, he placed the corn on the ground, careful not to make a sound. He then rose and disappeared behind the hut.

The moon now hung directly overhead. There came the muted roar of a vehicle passing on the main road and then the soft clanging of the iron bell in the district office as it rang twice. The sound spread throughout the subdistrict and the entire Blora area as wood and metal clubs marked the time. And then it was calm again, as calm as any village at night.

The gambler reappeared with a load of branches in his arms. "He's probably hungry," he said to himself as he carefully stacked the branches in a pile near the corn. "When he wakes, he'll have some grilled corn to eat. Oh, the suffering he must have gone through!" Sitting on the ground, he began to husk the ears of corn. The moon shone down upon him. His eyes disappeared into the shadow of his forehead.

The bell in the district office began to ring again. Then again and again as the contagious sound of alarm traveled through the Blora area. The air became a sea of sound, with waves of clanging and thumping disrupting its former stillness. The sound of alarm washed over the night.

"What kind of place is this getting to be?" the gambler grumbled. "People are trying to get some sleep and they're ordered to wake up. If it's not an air raid, it's something else! What are the Japanese up to now?" Husking the corn, he chuckled as he mumbled happily to himself. "He really is my son."

He placed the clean ears of corn in a pile at his right and set fire to the branches before him. As the flames grew, the kindling popped and crackled. Squatting beside the fire he began to roast the corn. The fire illuminated his aged and wrinkled face. He had neither a mustache nor a beard; a quarter of his hair was white. His eyes sparkled hazily in the firelight. The shadow of his body followed behind his every movement.

With the pounding of the drums, the night's calm disappeared. From every direction came the muffled hubbub of voices and human activity. Overhead the moon shone serenely. The sound of disparate cries slowly melded into one. The beating of many drums became a steady roll. Even as the gambler listened, the pounding began to fade and weaken, then finally die. Content, the gambler turned his corn, a soldier pleased with the spoils of his foray.

Just as he finished roasting his tenth cob of corn he heard the pounding of feet. "Where's the raid now?" The gambler cursed to himself. "I tell you, anything is possible with the Japanese. A man can't even sleep without being disturbed." The corn kernels hissed as they cooked.

The sound of footsteps became more distinct. The gambler put down the ear of corn he had been roasting and stood. He walked to the gate, where he peered to the right and the left and then returned to the hearth and the corn.

The wind brought him a muffled cry. "He's probably at his father's hut." The gambler jumped up and looked wildly around him. The sound of a wall in his hut being stretched and torn caused his head to jerk back. He heard the sound of corn stalks behind the hut being trampled and broken. The gambler listened more carefully. "Thunder and lightning!" he barked. "What was that?" He jumped to his left and ran to the side of the hut. Then he turned to search the right side before taking his place once more before the doorway. The light from the moon and the fire revealed the confusion on his face and the movements of a man not sure of what to do.

The sound of footsteps and voices grew louder. "Where's his father's hut?" someone cried.

"Up ahead!" came another cry.

The gambler whimpered softly in fear. "My boy, they're after my boy. They'll take you away if they find you. You're on the run again." He wanted to dive into the hut but his terror fixed him firmly in place.

"He's a traitor."

"An Allied spy," came the response.

"We've got Allied spies in Blora?"

"You can see for yourself later."

As the voices closed in a dog yelped as if it had been kicked. Suddenly the gambler awoke from his shock. He turned around and ran into his hut. The floor creaked beneath his weight. Then he stopped. The hut was empty. The beggar was no longer there. All he could see were the slivers of light from the fire outside that pierced the hut's wall and disappeared like shooting stars in a darkened sky. In the back wall of the hut, beneath the dancing stars of firelight, was a hole, and through the hole he saw the ground outside, pale beneath the yellow light of the moon.

The sound of pounding feet grew louder. The gambler suddenly thrust his hand out in a gesture, but then let it fall weakly to his side as he settled into a crouch on the floor. His head drooped. From outside came the sounds of human cries. "My son, my boy," he whispered. He was still as the wind picked up and the stars of firelight danced furiously on the walls. He poured out his confusion in a stifled moan. "Where are you? Are you alive? Will the Japanese hunt you forever? If you are my son, I pray to God that He always watches over you. Was it for nothing that I brought you into this world?"

He stood slowly and dragged himself out of the hut. He squatted at the hearth and went back to roasting his corn with apparent disinterest, as if nothing at all had happened. His face was a web of fine lines. The silver in his hair glistened in the firelight.

"On guard," he said to himself. "And I didn't even get a chance for a good look at his face."

He didn't move as the gate of his fence was kicked open. He saw eight watchmen with sharpened bamboo poles running down the path and through his field toward the hut but he hardly gave them notice. With his eyes focused on the fire, he tended his corn as if nothing were happening. From the pile of roasted cobs on the ground to his left, he chose an ear and began to eat.

The patrol stopped next to the hearth before him. They were dressed in loose-fitting black trousers and short-sleeved shirts. The tips of their bamboo spears, burned to a point and covered with castor oil, glistened in the firelight. The gambler stood slowly, chewing his corn. The flames illuminated the cruel lines that marked the faces of the men before him. The one closest to him—wearing brown rubber-soled boots that looked black in the dark—snapped at him, "Where's your son?"

"My son?" the gambler asked, feigning ignorance and surprise. "Did you say my son?"

The man closest to him glanced at the man behind him and signaled with his head. The latter walked toward the hut. The first turned again to the gambler. "Out with it!" he ordered. "Where is your son? Don't act stupid with us!"

"What are you talking about?"

"Commander Hardo, your son, traitor to the Japanese army."

"What can I say? I haven't seen him for half a year," the gambler said, his voice both friendly and sincere. "Have you had news of him? Is he in the Blora area?"

The gambler's questions and tone of his voice seemed to soften the leader's stance. "Yes," he replied. "We have word that he's in the area. We have information that he was seen tonight at around eight o'clock."

"Why are you looking for him here?"

"I just do what I'm told," the leader complained.

"Where was he seen?"

"I don't know. I'm just following the village chief's orders to look for him here. Are you sure that he's not been here?" he asked with displeasure.

"I don't think so."

"What do you mean you 'don't think so'?"

"I mean no!" he answered with certainty as he looked around to watch the man who was searching his hut. "No, he's not here," he reaffirmed for the leader.

The officer who had been searching the hut returned. "He's not there. But there's a hole in the wall big enough for a person to crawl through."

The gambler smiled. "Oh, that, I kicked it in my sleep."

"Search the field," the leader snapped, causing the other men to spread out through the field. The eyes of both the leader and the gambler followed the men. After they had disappeared into the field, the leader looked back at the former district head. "If I find out that you've hidden your son, I'm warning you, you'll take the responsibility!"

The former district head looked down at the hearth, now a shrunken pile of embers. "Fine," he said, a challenge, as he munched on his corn again.

"Your son is a troublemaker," the leader complained as he poked the tip of his sharpened bamboo pole into the ground. He then stared at the hole he had just made. "Here we are, up against the Allies, with the war coming our way and thousands of our young soldiers falling at the front and your son stabs us in the back! Wouldn't you describe that as treachery?" He blinked as he stared at the former district head but the latter gave no reply. "Isn't it?" he asked again, almost a threat. "Isn't it?"

The gambler's mouth fell open. "I suppose it is," he answered.

"You're his father, aren't you?" When the gambler nodded the leader went on. "And he's not here? And you really didn't see him?"

"No, I didn't, but I would like to ask you something." The gambler frowned as he looked at the leader. The man nodded as if to say go ahead. "I'd like to ask you something."

"What's that? Speak up!" the leader said, sure of his authority.

"What kind of clothes was he wearing?"

"I don't know," the leader answered irritably. "All I was told was to find Hardo, the former platoon leader. He's tall and dark and has a long scar on his right arm."

"Then I'm sure I didn't see him."

The leader turned to look in the direction of the fence and pointed at the gate. "Or maybe you saw someone walking along the path through the field over there?"

"I was cooking myself some corn. I had just woken from a dream. In my dream I was trying to fight off a rhino and I kicked out a hole in the wall. Then I woke up and cooked myself some corn. Alone." He looked over the shoulder of the officer at the fallen gate. "I didn't see anyone come in that way." He picked up another ear of corn and began to eat it with little concern. The leader frowned as he looked at the corn.

"I don't care about your dreams, your sleeping habits, or your corn. I asked if you had seen someone walking on the dike or near your hut."

"No, I didn't. I said that earlier, didn't I?" the gambler replied more strongly.

The two men stood face to face, neither saying a word. The gambler took another bite of corn and chewed it nonchalantly. When finished with the ear, he threw it into the field. The embers of the hearth between the men began to lose their glow. The gambler's feet were bare. The watchman wore not only rubber-soled boots but socks as well.

One by one, the patrol squad returned to gather around the dying hearth. Some wore shoes of goat skin that were already cracked and frayed. The splayed feet of the men who wore no shoes were dirty.

"There's no one in the field," one of the squad reported in a monotone to the leader as he looked over the gambler from head to foot with a dispassionate gaze.

Another of the returning men looked down at the feet of his unit leader and reported, "Outside the hole in the wall of the hut I found a set of footprints leading to the fence, and in that spot the fence is down." He lifted his head and looked at the gambler as well.

"I went out the hole earlier to relieve myself in the river. And then I gathered some branches to cook my corn," the gambler explained. "If you don't believe me, we can go measure them. That's if you don't believe me," he added, somewhat embarrassed but still friendly. "No one has been here except me. And you can see for yourself that I was cooking corn." He pointed at the ground and the pile of roasted corn. The leader's eyes followed his arm. "If you want to eat some, go right ahead. You're welcome to it."

The members of the unit looked at their leader, each with a question in his eyes. The leader seemed confused as he muttered, "Go ahead." He then bent down, picked up the largest ear of corn, and began to eat. The other men followed him and were soon smacking their lips as they ate. "He's not here," the unit leader said with his mouth full of corn. "We'll look for him somewhere else." He turned to the former district head, a warning in his eyes. "I hope you're not lying." Then he turned and began to walk away. Still chomping on their corn, the other men set off too.

The gambler followed the squad at a distance. The moon was moving westward. In the dim light the group of men before him looked like a flock of black birds. Leaving the gate, they turned to the left and soon disappeared from sight behind the tassels of corn. The gambler busied himself repairing the gate in his fence. After righting the gate he began to walk slowly back toward the hut.

Halfway along the path he stopped in sudden attention. The sound of a salutation in Japanese caused him to turn his head. He hurried his pace and made his way toward the hut, but before reaching the entrance he heard behind him the sound of the fence gate being kicked open again. He swung around and the tension he had felt earlier that night returned as he saw three men walking toward him. One, a Japanese officer, marched stiffly ahead of the others. He was followed by a small man dressed in white civilian clothing. The third man, farthest back, was a short squat Indonesian soldier.

The gambler stood beside the door to the hut, not far from the warm hearth, ready to greet his visitors. The

Japanese officer immediately placed his hands on his waist and shouted gruffly, "Are you the father of Raden Hardo, the former platoon leader?"

The gambler nodded quickly. The Japanese officer snarled and spat his displeasure. "I want answers. Proper answers!"

"*Hai.*" The gambler's voice trembled as he offered his consent in Japanese.

The Japanese officer came closer. "Good. Is he here?"

"No, sir." The gambler trembled.

"No?" the officer screamed. He took another step forward and swung his clenched fist at the gambler's cheek. The former district head staggered sideways. "I want the truth. The truth! Where is he?"

The former district head tried to right himself but stumbled as awkwardly as an untrained recruit. "I haven't seen him for half a year."

"I am not a child, understand? You tell me no fairy tales. Where is he? I want the truth!" He stepped toward the gambler. Glaring at the old man, he punched him with his left hand directly between the eyes.

"I don't know," the gambler cried as he stumbled backward toward the corn patch. Grabbing frantically, he pulled down three or four stalks as he fell to the ground. The other stalks waved and rustled around him. The gambler immediately picked himself up and walked back to the Japanese officer. "I don't know," he said again, this time with greater conviction.

The officer grumbled something in Japanese and then stepped into the hut. The man in civilian clothing turned to the gambler. "Weren't you once the district head of Karangjati?"

The gambler nodded slowly as his hand stroked his cheek and brow. The moonlight illuminated his pain.

"I replaced you," the man added but the gambler said nothing. "This isn't my doing," the new district head whispered. "It's the chief of Kaliwangan who's put everyone in an uproar. I wouldn't put it past him to have made it all up." He paused and whispered even more warmly, "Your son really isn't here?"

The former district head shook his head in disgust. The Indonesian soldier watching the scene had a look of pity in his eyes. When the gambler noticed the soldier, he smiled, a sign of trust.

The Japanese officer came out of the hut. The current district head stepped back slightly to let him by. The officer's attention was focused completely on the former district head of Karangjati. He studied him carefully from head to foot. "Watch it!" he warned angrily. "You know the military police. They'll have your neck! I want truth! Where is he?" He placed his left hand on his waist. His right hand clutched the hilt of his sword.

Still frightened, the gambler forced himself to answer. "I don't know."

"Watch it! You watch it!" the officer advised again as he turned and proceeded toward the gate.

The district head of Karangjati and the Indonesian soldier followed. Halfway to the gate, the soldier turned and nodded. The gambler returned the nod. And after the Japanese officer and the district head had stepped onto the path and turned to the right, the soldier hastily fixed the gate. Then he scurried away to catch up with his commanding officer. The three men disappeared from sight.

The gambler stood before the cold hearth. "So, it was you who made this mess," he whispered. He lifted his eyes from the gate to the moon. Ringed in hues of black and blue, his eyes watered. The moon floated in the heavens. "You betrayed your future son-in-law." He bowed his head to look at the hearth. "Just because my boy is a beggar now and not a Japanese slave, a respected Japanese slave. When he was an officer, weren't you proud of him then? You told everyone about it. But now? At one time, his every wish was your command, but now you hand him over to the executioner." He sat down on the threshold of his hut and whispered, "Of course, he must have stopped to see Ningsih." He stood and wept into his closed hands. "My son!" Like a madman he kicked the uneaten ears of corn and the ashes in his hearth. "My son!" he screamed again but then he fell silent, exhausted and out of breath. "Is this what my life is to be like?"

He turned suddenly and hurried into the hut. The woven bamboo floor creaked with his weight as he rolled about on his sleeping mat. "My son!" he called sadly. "My wife, my boy, myself." His body twisted in anger, disappointment, sadness, and fear. Finally, weakened, he pulled himself out of the hut and stumbled down the path toward the gate. His hair was tangled and wild-looking. "I want to gamble," he said excitedly as he reached the gate.

He threw the gate open. Scrambling out and to the left, he quickly vanished from sight.

Calm returned once more. The sounds of the bronze orchestra floated through the evening air, now much more clearly than before. The moon had edged its way farther toward the west. The wind rose and fell and the roof of the hut fluttered and whistled softly. A rooster crowed, the morning's first, and that was soon followed by another and then another in refrain. A quarter of an hour later the crowing too had died and it was quiet once more.

The bell in the district office pealed three times.

THREE

Darkness gathered beneath the bridge spanning the Lusi River to the east of Blora station, where the moonlight failed to penetrate. And beneath the bridge, where the riverbank rose to meet the descending frame, a row of people slept, apparently content, their chests rising and falling with regularity.

From the bridge descended the intermittent pounding of footsteps marking the passage of troops. Two, three automobiles passed, and with their unforgiving roar the sleepers mumbled curses as they drove on. After the commotion faded, silence returned once more, and the moon above the bridge slowly and silently began to set.

From the river a few dozen meters below there arose

the rippling sound of water slipping over stones, wend-
ing its way through the elephant grass and circling
around the pillars of the bridge. In the moon's shadow
beneath the bridge, the elephant grass on the riverbank
was black; in the moonlight, another patch of grass was
white. Across the river a wall of green bamboo rose upward, a grove of poles with strips of black missed by the
moon, and tassels that shook and swayed with abandon.
The dark shadow of the bridge curved down to the
water's edge, crossed the river, and rose again to disappear somewhere along the top of the opposite bank. In
the water the shadow rippled with the restless movement
of the river. The broken pilings of a forgotten bridge
stuck their heads a meter above the water. Against the
river's force, the poles bowed their heads downstream to
create triangles of trembling darkness in the water.

The bell in the district office pealed four times. The
sound of footsteps and automobiles passing over the
bridge disappeared, replaced by silence. Night's calm had
returned when suddenly the elephant grass beneath the
bridge began to move. From the grass a beggar emerged,
carefully made his way up the bank, and lay down on an
unoccupied patch of hard and barren ground among the
sleeping beggars.

The bell of the district office pealed once more and
was followed by a tumultuous sound at the station; fire-
wood was being loaded on the train. Then ten minutes
later came the hissing of steam passing through the ar-
teries of the locomotive. The early-morning calm of the
small city disappeared, to be replaced by the commotion
of day. Locomotives roared, whistled screamed, and engines moaned without respite. The switching of trains on
their tracks added to the noise.

"Son of a bitch!" One sleepy curse was soon followed by others as they passed from one mouth to an-

other. "Thunder and lightning!" Another curse carried across a cacophony of coughs and rumbling throats. The coughs seemed to percolate inside the beggars' chests but then stop before spouting from their mouths.

"Shit!" an old man spat.

The long scream of a locomotive suddenly pierced the air as a train began to roll across the trestle about twenty meters to the south. Another round of curses erupted with the final oath ending in ". . . your mother!" The row of bodies shifted their positions.

The noises showed no sign of diminishing. Black smoke, billowing from train stacks, rolled heavily upward to turn the sky to haze. Ten meters to the southwest of the bridge, a steam-driven water pump let out an enormous sigh which soon changed to a rumble and then a roar that overpowered even the wailing of the trains' engines. But the beggars no longer cared, and returned to the contentment of sleep.

The moon sagged heavily in the east as the new day's light began to pierce the horizon. With darkness gradually stripped away, the dawn brought the area around the bridge to life. People passed over the bridge; most were heading for the market. In time the rumble of footsteps grew louder as the number of feet passing over the bridge increased. The new day had arrived and slowly, beneath the bridge, the sunlight began to filter in.

Nine beggars, men and women, one by one began to awaken from their sleep. They sat up, shook, then coughed and cleared their throats. Soon all the beggars were awake save one, the newly arrived beggar, who continued to lie there. A chorus of coughs echoed in the chamber beneath the bridge. One by one the beggars picked themselves up and lamely made their way down the bank to disappear into the elephant grass and then reappear at the river's edge below. Beside the water they squatted to relieve themselves and then began to bathe.

Only the one beggar was now left beneath the bridge. He lay on the ground face upward. His legs were stretched out straight before him while his head nestled in the crook of a bridge piling. The first flies of the day appeared and began to buzz above his face. Even as the sound and noise from the station grew louder he remained intensely calm, apparently at rest and not in the least concerned with the world around him. A train whistled and a formation of cars proceeded across the trestle twenty meters to the south. In their windows were the faces of tradespeople just setting off to sell their wares in the Cepu market. And below the train, beneath the bridge, their waste lay scattered about—banana, teak, and other kinds of leaves that had been used as wrappers, many with bits of cake and food still clinging to them. Feathers and bones also lay scattered around a cold heap of charcoal and ashes, a hearth for many fires used to cook the scavenged carcasses of chickens, cats, and dogs.

The beggar opened his eyes for a moment, looked around, then closed them again before repositioning his body toward the north and continuing his sleep. Below him the elephant grass began to move again. From it a tall thin beggar appeared, stooping as he trudged slowly up the steep bank. As he approached the spot where the sleeping beggar lay, his eyes grew wide with attention. He knelt and then bent to look more closely. "Hardo!" he cried in delighted surprise.

The prone beggar stirred and twisted around to look at the man who was bending over him. He blinked, rubbed his eyes, and coughed before pulling himself into a sitting position. "Dipo, what are you doing here?" he asked as he yawned and stretched. He rubbed his red and watering eyes.

"Hardo!" Dipo cried again. He sighed with delight as he thrust his hand out to take Hardo's in his own. Dipo brushed the ground with his hand and sat down. "I thought they'd caught you last night."

"Caught me?" Hardo laughed. "Just about, just about, but they haven't caught me yet." With his forearm he wiped the tears from his eyes once more.

"I told you once"—Dipo's voice was stern—"that the only thing that's going to get you in trouble is a woman. And what happened last night could only have happened if you forgot my advice." As Dipo stretched, his ribs and breastbone protruded. The hair in his armpits seemed to stand erect. As he pulled, his lips into a taut, thin line, his unkempt mustache grew wider. "That's right, isn't it?" Dipo asked, seeking confirmation as he shifted his buttocks to lean against a bridge pillar.

"You still don't know me, Dipo." Hardo seemed to apologize as he spoke. "And never have been able to understand my feelings or know the beauty of memories that stand out so clearly and keep inviting me to relive them and to immerse myself with all my senses." Following Dipo's lead, he leaned against a steel guy line.

Dipo grimaced. "Shithead!" he swore in Japanese. "If you had any idea how afraid I was for you last night, you'd be ashamed to talk like that." He stretched his feet straight out on the ground. "Go wash yourself," he mumbled to Hardo.

Hardo pushed himself up, stood exhaustedly for a moment, and began to walk down the embankment. On his back, running at an angle, was the print of the steel line. As he disappeared into the grass, Dipo's eyes scanned the river and watched the swirling water as it rushed swiftly past. The river and its banks had begun to fill with people.

"Poor bastard," Dipo muttered. "But that's what

happens to someone who's always had it easy," he reasoned. "When all of a sudden he finds himself without, his beautiful memories become a sickness." He stared at Hardo, who was bathing in the river. "But who's to blame? People grow accustomed to what they have. So how can I blame him? Maybe he's right. Maybe not everyone would agree but it might be right for him. People get used to what they have; it's the same for everyone." He stared vacantly around him. His eyes studied the bend in the river to the north. There at the bend, where the banks were overgrown with towering stands of deep green bamboo, the river seemed to stop.

Looking back down at Hardo, he found that his friend had already finished bathing. "Poor bastard," he whispered again. "Look at what happened to his family because of us. Ruined . . . all because we failed."

Making his way up the embankment, Hardo disappeared into the thick fold of grass. When he reappeared his face was red from exhaustion.

"Poor bastard," Dipo repeated.

Water was still dripping from Hardo's back when he returned to his place beneath the bridge. His loincloth was dry but streams of water ran from his hair onto his shoulders. He sat down in the place where he had sat before. "What happened last night?" he asked.

"Shithead!" Dipo cursed. "You have to be more careful, Hardo. One by one dysentery has been attacking all our friends; now, if the military police were to get you. . . . They're not going to catch me, though. At least I don't have any scars. But you? With that scar on your arm, you're easy to spot."

Hardo looked at the long scar on his right arm and shook his head. He nodded and looked at his friend without comment.

"You know," Dipo continued in an instructive tone,

"that scar of yours is both your judge and executioner. The mark that Japanese bayonet left will be your eternal misfortune. It's the one and only decoration the Dutch East Indies has given you in recognition of your service." Hardo laughed. "I think now that when you were in the civil guard defending Surabaya, it wasn't much different from someone trying to save a poisoned goat that was already in its death throes. Hey . . ." He seemed to remember something. "Have you had anything to eat?"

"Eat? Last night I drank a lot of river water," Hardo answered weakly.

"So you're still keeping your vow?"

"Yes," Hardo answered shortly. "And will do so until Karmin turns himself over and confesses his treachery to me. Until he comes back to our side."

Dipo grunted. The bridge vibrated with the passing of people, horses, buffalo, cows, and vehicles. The number of people crossing the bridge, both from the east and the west, had grown. So too had the number of people coming down to the river to bathe. Young boys tending buffalo and cattle led their animals into the water to scrub their backs with makeshift brushes of grass stalks and weeds. Women washed clothing, rice for the next meal, corn, and their own bodies as well. Young children played in the yellow water around them.

A hen approached but ignored the seated men. Scratching the ground, it called its chicks, which came scurrying up to their mother to peck at the loosened soil.

The beggars watched the hen and its chicks. "Yes, I'm keeping my vow," Hardo repeated. His voice was serious. "I will not eat anything that nature itself does not provide."

"You may be the epitome of the mysterious Oriental but until you can control your feelings about your fiancée . . ."

"I know, I know." As Hardo gazed down toward the dancing river, his face took on a sudden glow. He smiled as he came to his own defense. "Part of our life we give to sentiment, another part to wisdom, another part to stupidity. That's how life goes, but after all of that, we give ourselves to death. Everyone's life is like that."

"But in this kind of situation, here and now," Dipo argued, "there's no room for sentiment, not even a little. And if you can't control your feelings, you're not going to live another four hours!"

"I know you mean well, Dipo. I know you're thinking of my safety. I appreciate that, but you also must remember that a man can't always be strong. Don't you think so?" As if embarrassed by his question, Hardo bowed his head and scratched his fingers on the ground. "Just when a person is at his weakest, that's when sentiment comes. And it strikes as swiftly as a sword."

"The hell with that!" Dipo cut him off. "Your head is in a cloud. It's that kind of talk I can't stand. You got that? Lift up your head, stick out your chin, pretend you're training a new batch of recruits. Face forward! Open your eyes! Prick up your ears! Shout it out: Do that, do this!" He looked silently at his friend but Hardo's head remained bowed. "Have you forgotten your oath as a soldier?" He watched his friend's lips but Hardo would not look up; he continued picking at the ground with his hand. "You're a soldier and will always be a soldier. You might be able to shuck off the promise you made as a soldier to the Japanese, but you can't ignore the promise you made as a soldier in Sampur Cave. Don't even try! Raise your sword when you have to; shoot when you have to shoot. After that . . . only then, when you're free from your duties as a soldier, will no one stop you from tasting your girlfriend's lips."

Dipo watched Hardo's hand tracing patterns on the

ground. Then his eyes turned to the hen that was now moving away from them and making its way farther down the bank.

"And last night . . ." Dipo began. Hardo stopped scratching to look at him. ". . . our former unit leader came down here beneath the bridge with the district head from Karangjati. No, not your father. You've heard about that, haven't you? That your father was fired?"

Hardo nodded weakly and watched the scab-scarred arms of his friend and their wild gesticulations as he spoke.

"Yes. And Karmin too, Platoon Commander Karmin!"

"Karmin?" Hardo uttered in surprise. Dipo nodded in confirmation. "So you got away from the unit leader and Karmin?"

"Of course, of course I did," Dipo laughed with victorious pride.

Hardo's eyes widened; his mouth hung slightly open. "How did you do it? Here you are, the height of an elephant. What did you do? Turn yourself into a pole?"

The hands of the two men, cupped on the ground, resembled frogs waiting for mosquitoes. Dipo smirked before continuing. "I dropped one shoulder like this and curled up my right hand. I looked like a crippled buffoon!" Dipo hooted. His body shook with laughter. Hardo laughed too. "Don't believe it," Dipo said arrogantly. "They're not as dangerous as you might think. What's dangerous is your sentimentality, the conditions your men have to live in, and that scar on your right arm." He traced the slash mark on Hardo's arm with an authoritative gesture.

"What did they say?" Hardo asked calmly, his eyes on Dipo. Dipo laughed. His face shone with the recounting of his successful escape from the unit leader and Karmin.

"From what the chief of Karangjati said I gathered it was none other than your future father-in-law, the head-man of Kaliwangan, who reported you!" Dipo stopped to look at Hardo. As if kicked in the stomach, Hardo cramped his body inward. "So I hope now, Hardo, that you'll stop being so sentimental." His voice was low and sympathetic.

Hardo's eyes traced the span of the bridge to the other side of the river, and he sighed. "I guessed as much," he said sadly.

"Stop that sentimental crap!" Dipo reminded him harshly. "How many times do I have to tell you? Ten, twenty?"

Hardo stared at Dipo. "You don't have to insult me," he said bitterly.

Dipo shot back his reply. "Well, when a person won't follow good advice and won't face facts, then maybe he should be insulted!"

Hardo refrained from further comment and sat in silent thought. Dipo continued. "By now, the men who've been caught have probably had their heads cut off in Jakarta. The Japanese would do it in Gambir Park where people used to like to stroll on the promenade. So please Hardo, don't give them a chance to increase their tally." His voice was sympathetic but insistent. "And Karmin last night"—Hardo grasped Dipo's arm—"Karmin told the others that *he's* probably not here and that it would be better to detain the village chief until they determined whether there was any truth to his report."

"That was last night he said that?"

"Yes, but then the district head said, 'No, we can't do that. But we could arrest his father.' The unit leader looked furious but said nothing. God, he must hate you,

Hardo! It was you, you remember, who challenged him to a sparring match and then wiped his ass. After that, from what the district head said, I found out that they have a spy in place at Ching's gambling house. I don't know who Ching is but he must be Chinese. That doesn't mean he's against us though. Have you seen your father?"

"My father . . ." Hardo stuttered. "Yes, I even spoke with him for a while but not for very long; the watchmen and the youth corps raided his hut."

"But you got away."

"Yes, I got away."

"Maybe it was your father who betrayed you. How did you know about your father's place?"

"I just happened on it."

"Your father's getting on in years, isn't he? He wouldn't hold up under torture. I suggest that you be careful, Hardo!"

Hardo shook his head weakly. "That's impossible," he said as if to reassure himself. "He would never betray me. He didn't even know who I was." He spoke sadly, "I lost my mother because of our rebellion. I don't want to lose my father too."

"My God! What are you talking about?" Dipo interjected. "Look at what you're up against. You have the choice of a sword or, if the executioner's arm is tired, a bullet through your brain. And you're worried about your father? Right now, he doesn't exist! I'm serious. The only thing you should be thinking about is your men, who are God knows where and have a great deal more suffering to contend with than does your father."

The scream of a train whistle was followed by silence. And then, a moment later, a line of cars passed over the trestle from the direction of Cepu.

"You have to stop being sentimental," Dipo insisted once more, an order for Hardo, who continued to scratch the ground with his fingers. In his scratch marks the shape of a pistol began to emerge. "You fought against the Japanese in Surabaya when the East Indies were falling. For that the Japanese put you in Mojokerto Prison for a year. As an Indonesian volunteer you went up against them again. And you're still fighting, even now. For God's sake, Hardo, by this time you should be a model soldier! Forget your fiancée and your father." His ears pricked up at the sound of shouting from the station. "Right now we don't have the time or the space left in our minds to worry about other people. You have to think about yourself. So what do you feel about Karmin now?"

"No different," Hardo answered coolly. He lifted his hand and ran it through his hair.

"You still defend him?"

"Yes."

"Then you're crazy. We have to capture him; I'll agree with you on that, but after that I don't agree with you at all." Dipo stared silently at Hardo. "That's weakness on your part." He suddenly roared with laughter. "We'll capture him and if you can't do it, then I'll cut off his head. Think of it, Hardo. Ten of our men had their heads cut off in Jakarta. Isn't that sign enough of his treachery?"

Hardo lifted his eyes and watched Dipo as he laughed. The blood rushing to Dipo's head caused the tips of his ears to darken. Dipo's long beard brushed across his breastbone. "My feelings are not a sign of weakness," was Hardo's wistful comment.

As Dipo laughed the hairs of his mustache stood erect. "The hell it's not," he whispered with certainty. "That's a bunch of crap!"

Hardo looked to the sky, reluctant to listen to more of Dipo's talk. He turned his head toward the sound of footsteps on the bridge. "It appears to me, Dipo, that I'm more famous around here than you!" He bowed his head and placed his left leg over his right. "But maybe that's because I'm from this area."

"And that's why, my friend, your biggest enemy is your own sentimentality."

The blood rushed to Hardo's face. "Maybe so," he mused bitterly, but then calmed himself enough to ask, "What did Karmin say after that?" He listened intently for Dipo's answer.

"Karmin suggested that they arrest the chief of Kaliwangan and keep an eye on your father. When the unit leader asked if your fiancée should be detained Karmin said that wouldn't be necessary."

"Did he really?"

Dipo nodded in agreement, but then reminded Hardo: "Don't you see now—how because of your feelings, that ridiculous sentimentality of yours—how many people you've got involved. Maybe you haven't heard about your fiancée?" Dipo watched Hardo for his reaction.

Hardo bowed his head.

"I've known about it since yesterday afternoon," Dipo added.

Hardo's attention was suddenly focused on Dipo's words. A sense of excitement loomed quietly in his eyes.

"I know what you're thinking, Hardo. You want to find out about her. I can read your face like an open book!"

Hardo dropped his head again. "Yes, I do," he mumbled awkwardly.

"Your fiancée"—Dipo raised his arm to point; Hardo lifted his head again—"lives only sixty meters from here." He dropped his hand again.

"But what did the unit leader say?" Hardo asked, avoiding the subject of Ningsih.

"He suggested that your father, your fiancée, and her father the chief be detained until such time as you've been captured or have had your head cut off in Jakarta. Only then would they be released."

Both Dipo and Hardo pondered this thought. A light morning wind began to blow and stir the tips of the bamboo. The grove whispered as it swayed. The crowd in the river had thinned and from the bend, beside the bamboo grove, came the chattering of lizards, like voices from an outdoor café.

"It's a pity we didn't get to know Karmin's true colors before he betrayed us," Dipo complained, "and turned us into hunted animals." He stood, stretched, and sat again. He stroked his beard, pulling his hand down its length, like a mendicant priest. He sat erect, placing none of his weight on the bridge piling, but then reclined on the scattered mat of limp and faded leaves. Flies hovered around him as he spoke. "On a morning like this it would be great to have a cup of coffee, just like we used to, a good cup of coffee. Think about it, Hardo. Wouldn't a cup of coffee be nice?"

Hardo shook his head. "What else did you hear them say?"

"What else? Hmmm . . . I couldn't really see their faces, but with their lights they searched the area and checked the arms of some of those who hadn't left. They didn't say anything special, but clearly it was Karmin who carried the most influence. He got the unit leader to change his mind but, no, I can't think of anything special!"

Hardo ignored Dipo's comments. "But what did Karmin say?"

"That you might be jealous of him." Dipo seemed to be testing Hardo.

Hardo refused to become engaged. "What did he say?" he asked again.

"Karmin told the unit leader that it would be better not to arrest the woman. Wouldn't be chivalrous, he said. And the fool praised Karmin for this blather. He said that Karmin was truly valiant, with the blood of a warrior in him." The two men laughed. "I think we should do something about Karmin. Sooner rather than later," Dipo added. "He has a great deal of influence with the Japanese and even more with his own men. But he's a blight that must be gotten rid of." Dipo spat on the ground. His taunting voice seemed to demand a response. "And you're jealous of him?"

Hardo ignored the question. "So the military police didn't come along last night?"

"No, and I was a little surprised that they didn't. But, but . . . God, I'm hungry. Aren't you hungry?"

"No!"

"That's right. You have that promise you made to feed you. That's fine for you maybe, but not for me. I'd never do such a thing, never."

"Come on. What else did they say?" Hardo continued his search for clues.

"After that they left; that's all. But I tell you, they certainly did get out all the recruits for this raid." He raised his arms and knitted his hands behind his head to form a pillow. "And weren't all the people down here bitching about it! I was here too and I tell you, for a moment there, I was scared. And I started to swear at them too."

"And me?" Hardo snorted.

"What do you mean?" Dipo asked.

"I was almost caught, you know."

"That was your own fault." He pulled his hands from beneath his head and rested their heels on the ground beside him. "What would you think if we just got rid of Karmin?"

"No." Hardo's voice was serious.

"No?" Dipo raised his upper body and sat up to look at his friend. "After all the harm he's done?"

"Think of him as sick, Dipo! And that his actions are those of a sick man, a reaction to his illness. You can't judge him for that. He doesn't know what he's doing. And there's no reason to hate him—"

"What?" Dipo said angrily. "You can rationalize all you want"—his face reddened as he frowned—"but you've got your head in the clouds! You're supposed to be a model soldier and maybe you are. Maybe you can do what's required of you but I doubt it, not until you stop your dreaming."

"Shut up!" Hardo snapped. Dipo rested against the piling and closed his eyes, listening to Hardo speak as a young woman might listen to her fiancée's plans for their future. "Listen to me. You're a model soldier, an ace of a soldier, and maybe you'll be a general someday what with the guts it took for you to rise up and fight and the bravery you needed to escape. But . . ." Dipo stared at Hardo. "But Karmin's not like that. He's sick. I know him. I've known him since we were kids. I know him well. He's a good and honest man. And loyal too! Maybe we are suffering the consequences of what he did or didn't do. But treachery, if that's what it was, doesn't last forever. People can change. Is there really anyone who is completely evil?"

Dipo remained silent as he raised his knees before leaning back against the girder again. His features were flushed with disgust as he tried with difficulty to remain calm and listen to Hardo's defense. His eyes wandered over the panorama before him, resting momentarily on the bamboo that lined the top of the riverbank and swayed in the morning wind. He traced the course of the river below where the children washed their buffalo and cattle. Leaving the water, they climbed the far bank where young women made their way up and down with baskets of sand at their waists. He followed a line of children who were now setting out for school on the opposite road.

"I know him well," Hardo stressed again. "And yes, before our little failure of a rebellion, maybe he did betray us. But you have to remember, Dipo, that if he betrayed us he did so without realizing it."

"Rubbish," Dipo muttered before retreating into silence once more.

"Listen to me," Hardo pleaded. "You knew that he was engaged, didn't you?"

"Is this story time?" Dipo asked coldly.

"Yes, it is, and you have to listen," Hardo told him.

"And I suppose you can force me to listen to your rationalizations?"

Hardo ignored the challenge. "Hear me out, would you? Karmin was engaged. I knew that. You knew that too. But what you and I didn't know and what he had only then found out was that his fiancée had run off and married the party chief of the region."

"And that's why he became a traitor?" Dipo was skeptical.

"Yes, that's why he became a traitor, but he did so completely unaware."

"That's a bunch of sentimental nonsense, my friend," Dipo advised. "His girl leaves him so he becomes a traitor. Does that make sense!?"

"Yes, it does."

"And that's why you defend him?"

"Yes."

"Sentimental crap! Hopeless garbage."

"Maybe."

"So now I know why. You're only defending him because you're in love too. That's the real reason."

"Listen, will you!" Hardo said with mounting anger. "Whether I'm sentimental or not, that's my business. But even you have to admit that love is an important part of a person's life."

Hardo ignored Dipo's cynical laughter. "Love is an important part of life and because of what happened to Karmin, all his hopes were crushed. The very foundation on which he had built his hopes suddenly disappeared. And, whether conscious of it or not, he wanted to inflict pain, to make everyone else feel that same loss. By coincidence we were the ones that he betrayed." Hardo's stare caused Dipo to draw a deep breath. "Maybe he is a traitor. No one's going to argue with you about that. And I know that there's nothing more common in this world than revenge. But in the end, all it does is perpetuate an endless cycle of the same."

"You're forgetting yourself and who you are," Dipo reminded him. "You're a soldier! You can't be a dreamer forever."

Hardo closed his eyes and spoke patiently. "Can't you shut up and listen for once? The Dutch East Indies were supposed to be so strong but the Japanese brought the country to its knees in a matter of days. Think of that. Japan is now in power but someday, as you yourself know—with the war getting closer—Japan is going to fall. But the promise of independence that the Japanese gave us has created a national awareness and someday, who knows . . ."

"You're dreaming, Hardo!" Dipo kept his eyes closed as he spoke.

"Shut up, Dipo, just shut up!" Hardo screamed. Dipo suddenly opened his eyes to fully reveal the disgust on his face. "We need Karmin's strength, his influence, his ability, and his men. The war is getting closer. The Japanese can scream all they want about a land war," he chuckled, "but Balikpapan has fallen and Surabaya is under daily attack. Not too long, not too long from now Japan is going to face judgment day. And when that happens we are going to take this country back. It will be an apocalypse."

At the upper corner of the bridge a thin pair of legs appeared. Dipo and Hardo's eyes widened as they descended the embankment. The legs grew longer until finally, the torso and head of a male beggar appeared. His body, from neck to calves, was wrapped in frayed, soiled rags. A small sleeping mat hung from the man's left shoulder. In his right hand was a coconut shell, his begging bowl. He stooped as he proceeded under the bridge toward the spot where they were seated. Almost beside them he lay down and closed his eyes. He was asleep in a second.

"It's Kartiman," Hardo whispered.

"I know," Dipo confirmed. "He's one I'll never forget." The two men studied the beggar's face with its crust of dirt and dust. Dipo, crouched over the man like a frog, frowned, and looked intently at him. "He must be exhausted."

"It really is Kartiman," Hardo said again with greater certainty, his doubts vanishing with the furrows on his brow. Hardo nudged the waist of the sleeping beggar with his hand. "Hey!" The beggar opened his eyes. "Hey, how are you?" Hardo asked.

Without reply, the beggar closed his eyes again and crossed his arms over his face.

"Let him sleep for a while," Dipo suggested to Hardo. "Anyway, what other thoughts do you have on Commander Karmin?"

"I still believe that I can make him see what he did wrong and come back to us. For God's sake, Dipo, at least give me the chance to try before you take care of him. He can be useful to us. Can't you see that?" Dipo ignored the hopeful gleam in Hardo's eyes. His own eyes focused on the tip of the sleeping beggar's nose.

"Put things in proportion and accept them for what they are," Hardo added cautiously. "Say whatever you like about what he did, but you have to admit his use. The war is getting closer, it's coming to us, here, to the place we're sitting and to the places we always thought were safe. Think of what the Allied forces will do. They would certainly make use of Karmin! Japan might scream but in the end, it's going to lose. That's certain. Even now, the Allies are taking the islands back from them. Japan can call the Atlantic Charter a worthless scrap of paper floating somewhere in that ocean but I for one believe there's still some strength left in it." He nodded his head. "It's every nation's right to—"

Dipo erupted in laughter. Flies darted away from him and his broad mouth as his jaw moved up and down. The tips of his ears darkened with his pulsing blood and his eyes became slits as his body shook. A convoy of freight cars from the direction of Rembang advanced toward the station, their loud rattle a counterpoint to Dipo's laughter. Kartiman, the sleeping beggar, opened his reddened eyes momentarily and shut them again.

"Why are you laughing?" Hardo asked puzzled.

"Asshole!" Dipo swore loudly and laughed again.

"Dreamer! What a dreamer you are!" he hooted and laughed again.

Hardo's body seemed to shrink from Dipo's laughter. Reluctant to repeat his question, he looked on, confused.

"Dreamer!" Dipo said again as his laughter began to subside. "Forget such dreams, my friend! The important thing, the most important thing we have to do is to take care of our men, all the ones who've been scattered, and to rebuild them into a cohesive fighting force. We have to roll up our shirtsleeves, even if we don't have shirts!" At this he chuckled and his body began to shake.

Hardo ignored Dipo's comments and let his eyes wander to the bend in the river to the north. He squinted his eyes and then squinted again. His taut mouth softened into a small smile.

Dipo's laughter finally died. "We are all soldiers," he whispered. "And if you think you can still trust Karmin and are still as sure of him as you once were, then go ahead with your plans, but do them by yourself."

"I want to contact Ningsih."

"That's too risky."

"But if she loves me, she'll want to help me."

"Dreamer!" he spat and then laughed again. "You'll get caught. Is that what you want? You're looking for trouble and I want no part of it."

The two men sat in silence like enemies. Neither moved as they pondered their secret thoughts. On the ground beside them Kartiman snored in safe contentment. Hardo grasped the steel guy wire above him, a pained expression on his face. Gazing up at the sky over the bridge, Dipo seemed to be in prayer. A frown settled on both men's faces. In the distance the water pump roared. The bridge shook with the intermittent passage of carts and wagons, its reverberations enlivening the pillars and guy wires. The river was quiet, its sand-colored water flowing nervously to the south over its rocky bed. Food wrappers tossed from the bridge floated down through the air to land in the tall grass on the bank. Others fell into the water. Drawn by the river's pull they floated slowly away toward the south. Occasional drops of spittle passed through the air to join the watery course. The two men sat absorbed in their thoughts.

Now that the sun was level with the tops of the bamboo, the cavity beneath the bridge began to absorb the light. A ray falling on Kartiman illuminated the tip of his nose. His sleeping body was painted with strips of dark and light. The beams and pillars of the bridge, rusted except for the spots where the paint still held or where caked with a layer of mud, now took on a reddish hue.

The noise from the station rose and fell. The roar of the pump stopped, and from somewhere nearby came the wheezing of a locomotive filled to the top with water. Drops of water splashed into the river.

Kartiman remained fast asleep. His eyes and his mouth quivered slightly as flies hovered around him. His arms lay on his stomach and his right leg, which was pulled up, formed a sharp angle because of its thinness. The torn rags that wrapped his body were held together here and there with pineapple fiber.

Finally, Dipo began to speak once more. "I don't think there's much use in hoping for help from Karmin. He's gotten too used to luxury. He'd kill himself before he'd stoop to live like this. He just wouldn't. He's like a rich country that's not about to forfeit its colonies."

"But listen to me, would you?" Hardo spoke patiently. "Think of him as ill. Think of him as having malaria. If a man has malaria you can't hate him just because he shivers."

"But you're a soldier!" Dipo clenched his fist and pounded it into the palm of his left hand. "You should know what that means and always be mindful of it." He stood and stretched. "I have to take a piss," he said, leaving Hardo and walking down the embankment to disappear into the elephant grass.

Hardo moved closer to Kartiman. "It really is Kartiman," he said to himself.

Kartiman straightened his legs. His arms fell from his stomach to his sides. His eyelids fluttered for a moment. Then he rolled his body to the left. "I'm so tired," he mumbled. "My whole body aches." Hardo watched him more closely. Kartiman moaned weakly. "Twice the watchmen caught me and beat me. The fuckers! They kicked me in the back with their shoes. How much do the Japanese pay them to make them want to kick people?" He rolled to the right, putting his back to Hardo, then turned to the left and back to the right again. Finally he opened his bloodshot eyes. The thick welts on his chest, visible through his open shirt, were proof of the torture he had undergone. His breastbone and ribs protruded. He reached out and took Hardo's hand in his own. "I don't suppose you know, Hardo . . ." He paused and glanced in the direction Dipo had gone. "No, I guess you wouldn't. Your father was arrested last night . . . at the gambling house."

"My father?"

"Yes, your father."

"What time was that?" Hardo's voice remained calm but his eyes stared intently at his friend. "Are you sure you weren't seeing things."

"Seeing things?" Kartiman questioned. "He was in the same cell."

"What time was that?" Hardo stared more closely.

"This morning, around three thirty. It was around five they released me with another kick in my back."

Hardo took a deep breath. Stillness hung in the air beneath the bridge. Hardo's eyes, momentarily wild, found their peace once more. His body, instantly tense, became relaxed. "Where were you arrested?" he asked finally.

"There," Kartiman pointed to the west. "Near the district office building."

"How many others did they arrest?"

"I don't know. I don't even know why I was arrested. All they did was look at my arm. I heard one of the police say, 'Tall and dark,' and then watched as all of his men turned their eyes on me. 'He fits,' that's what he said after that. One of them was reading from a piece of paper. He said, 'A five-centimeter scar on his right arm.' They checked my right arm and then the policeman who had arrested me kicked me in the back. Before I was interrogated I met your father in the cell and he told me that he had been accused of hiding you. I assumed therefore that it was you they were looking for. So I guess you hadn't heard anything?" Hardo didn't reply. "We have to get out of this place soon."

Hardo laughed. "The raids are over now. And besides," he said, "given how little the Japanese pay the men, they're not going to look too hard or too long. Are you sure my father was arrested?" he asked again in disbelief.

"I saw him myself! And he told me they found footprints leading from his hut to the riverbank. But that at the river they lost the track. That's what he told me. And this is for your information only. There's no need to tell Dipo about this. You know how he gets about family news. I suppose it's because he has no family of his own."

"Thanks, Kartiman," Hardo murmured appreciatively, then paused. Kartiman fell silent too. Noticing Dipo climbing up the bank, Hardo asked quickly, "Do you have any other news?"

"Yes, big news," Kartiman answered with sudden cheer.

"What is it?"

"This one can wait until Dipo gets here." They turned to watch the grassy bank. Below them the tall grass began to move. Dipo emerged and the two men waited as he made his way toward them, sat down, and leaned back against the bridge pillar.

Dipo wearily squeezed his eyes shut. His dark, dull skin was covered with blotches. His eyes sat deep in their hollows and his cheeks, almost his entire face, was covered with hair, giving him the appearance of an old monkey. Finally catching his breath, he spoke slowly. "Well, Kartiman, how are you?"

"Fine, just fine, same as always." He chuckled as he spoke. "How long have you been living here under the bridge?"

"Two days," Dipo replied. "Just two days. I got here on the fifteenth to wait for you. Did you bring us any news?"

Kartiman shifted his body back slightly until his head almost touched the piling. The glow in his eyes was that of a messenger of good tidings. He crossed his legs and rested his hands on his lap. He then made a fist with his right hand and raised it to his chin. "I have great news!" Dipo and Hardo's eyes blinked as they watched him. "Last night I was in Jepon, almost five kilometers from here, sleeping in the doorway of a Chinese shop. The moon was full and there I was all alone trying to keep myself warm. . . ." He paused to see if his audience was paying him the proper amount of attention. Hardo and Dipo sat poised and erect. "And I was feeling so incredibly sad, like I didn't have the strength left to fight for the life of this crippled movement of ours. But then . . ." Hardo and Dipo leaned toward Kartiman as if there were an electric force pulling them. "But then right when I was trying to add up the pros and cons of this kind of life, I saw off in the west the weak glow of a bicycle light. As the bicycle approached, I heard its bell ringing and a voice calling out my name. 'Kartiman!' At that I sat right up. And you know who it was? My brother, my older brother, the one who works as a mail carrier." Kartiman unclenched his fist and let his hand drop to the ground. "The first thing he said was, 'So you weren't making up stories about where to find you!' And then he whispered to me, 'Hey, little brother, you can't stop the world from turning.' And then he hugged me real hard and this surprised me. Yes, I know he loves me, and we're always hugging each other. Ever since we were kids, after our parents died, we didn't have anyone else. . . . But anyway, this hug was extra hard and with his voice shaking he said to me, 'Your troubles are over. Japan has surrendered!'"

Dipo's entire body shook as he suddenly roared in laughter, but with Hardo and Kartiman staring at him silently he slapped his scabby hand over his mouth. With his left hand he clutched the steel wire above Hardo's head. After his laughter subsided he shouted: "Shithead! What's that you're saying, shithead?" Then, quite suddenly, he fell silent as if embarrassed by his outburst.

"Don't you believe me?" Kartiman asked him. "Or you?" he said to Hardo, who was also glaring at him.

"Tell me what else he said," Hardo demanded.

"Well, I'm not sure. I mean, I don't know whether to believe it or not myself but my brother said that according to the telegram he intercepted from Jakarta, Indonesian nationalists have begun to move and take over the reins of power." Kartiman looked silently at his two superiors. "Japan is beaten! Japan has surrendered!"

A tense silence enveloped them. The three men bowed like wilted flowers, their lips not moving, their features expressionless save for their eyes, which shone brightly, like oil lamps burning beneath a full moon. The silence was pervasive; no movement interrupted the stillness. No sound was loud enough to invade their hearing. The earth at which they stared no longer existed. Emptiness was complete, a tense and silent void. No sound emanated from the passing feet overhead or from the plodding hooves of animals. A driver's flailing whip froze in midair. Litter tossed off the bridge by passersby hung motionless in the air, unable to proceed in their realm.

Kartiman lifted his head, his chest rising and falling. He stretched his hands high into the air and released a long cry before wrapping his arms around his two friends. For a moment the three men pressed their bodies tightly together as if hoping they might join into one and their hearts become a single unit. Sound once more vanished as the three men huddled like kittens in the cold.

Finally the men released each other to relieve themselves of the stifled sighs in their chests. The men's eyes shone brightly but—as if lacking the courage—they could not look at each other. Hardo stood and took a few measured steps to the edge of the bridge's shadow. He clutched the rusted pillar and stared at the river flowing silently below him. Kartiman, his nose gleaming in the sunlight, leaned back on his elbows. His jaw was slack as he breathed in and exhaled. Dipo stared silently at the white sky overhead. The three men didn't hear the two shrill whistles of a passing train.

Hardo suddenly turned and looked at Dipo. "Now what do we do?" he asked as he sat down near him.

Dipo pursed his lips, sucked in a gulp of air, and then blew it out through his mouth.

"Well?" Kartiman inquired.

Dipo shook his head. "The Japanese army is still strong. What strength do we have?"

"You sound like you're giving in," Hardo said accusingly.

"Leave me alone!" Dipo snapped. His eyes bulged as he stared at Hardo. "It wouldn't take a genius to figure that out, would it? Look at the shape our organization is in. Can't you see that? Shit, you can't even see that goddamned Karmin for what he is! And you would protect him too. Give in? Me?" He laughed again. "The Japanese army is still firmly on its feet and the volunteer troops and commander Karmin are still scouring the Blora area for you! We could be attacked at any moment. Jakarta might be burning, but here . . . here"—he stuck his finger in the ground—"it's the Japanese army!" His voice was shrill. "And the Japanese here have not announced their surrender."

The bell in the district office began to ring and from the direction of the station came the sound of people's shouts. The three men listened to the thuds of running feet, then looked at each other silently, intently aware of the pealing bell and the voices.

"The patrols are being called out again," Hardo said slowly.

"The Japanese army is still in power. That should be proof enough for you," Dipo said cynically. "And even if it's only half an hour before they announce their surrender, it could still mean the end for us."

"What do you think they're doing now?" Kartiman asked his two superiors.

Dipo looked calmly at Hardo, who stood, stiffly

erect before him. He then shifted his gaze to Kartiman and whispered, "We have to hide."

Kartiman rose and Dipo began to make his way slowly down the embankment, the two other men following. Like a cat after its prey, the two men followed stealthily behind, shouldering their way into the patch of green and yellow and brown elephant grass. For a moment, Hardo turned around. His eyes were fierce as he gazed at the white sky. But slowly his body was enveloped by the grass. His thighs first and then his stomach. Soon his neck and then his head were lost from sight. The stately stalks of grass swirled and swayed and then were still again.

The pealing of the district office bell was picked up in all directions. But beneath the bridge it was calm. There was no movement whatsoever. The bells continued their chant, and soon from atop the bridge came the sound of soldiers running. The shadows of the men stretched downward to fall on the river's opposite bank. Then they rose to fly, like quick black lines, across the water, disappearing in the grass and reemerging on the other bank before soaring to disappear from sight. Flakes of rust fell from the bridge. Drops of spittle sprayed through the air to land between the shadow of the bridge and the sunny patch of earth where Hardo had rested. At the bend in the river the tops of the bamboo lining its sides waved in the wind, their deep green leaves releasing a gentle rustle.

The mother hen that had that morning scoured the ground beneath the bridge returned. Scratching and clucking as it moved, the hen was soon joined by its chicks, each of them no larger than a fist, running helter skelter behind their mother, scratching and pecking as well. The hen scratched the soil in one spot, then moved on. It fell back slightly to turn over a discarded palm wrapper. The chicks raced from the spot where they had been pecking to peck at the leaf and turn it over and back again and again. Gradually the clutch made its way to the north of the bridge to disappear among the young bamboo.

In the distance, beneath the bamboo grove, a lizard called. From the south a fisherman appeared and found himself a place in the shade of the bridge. He draped his net over the steel guy wire, placed his catch basket on the ground, and then slowly sat down. He pulled from his headcloth a flint and stone, which he struck, igniting a spark that fell onto his readied tinder. When the tinder burst into flame he took from his headcloth a corn-leaf cigarette, lit it, and began to smoke. He watched the clear blue smoke that flew from his nose and mouth disappear in the wind.

At the upper right corner of the bridge one leg and then another appeared and began to make their way down the earthen slope. The figure of a female beggar carrying a baby in a sling. The woman proceeded directly to the fisherman, sat down in front of him, and stared at him expectantly, her eyes flashing back and forth between the man and his catch basket. Her lips moved but she said nothing. The fisherman sighed and stood. Taking his net, he walked away to the north leaving the woman behind.

The beggarwoman stared upward, her eyes brimming with a beggar's unanswered hope. She then bowed her head, looked at her baby in its sling, and swore. "Little bastard. You don't give me a moment of peace!" She pulled out her left breast and gave it to her child to suckle. The baby, with little flesh on its bones and a disproportionately large head, resembled more a giant tadpole than a human child.

As the child suckled, a few dozen young men, an auxiliary patrol squad, appeared at the right corner of the bridge and began to pick their way down the slope. All of the men wore black fezlike hats. "There's usually lots of 'em around here," the squad leader commented while looking at the lone beggarwoman with a child at her breast. He addressed the woman in a rough tone of voice. "Hey, have there been any male beggars around here?"

The woman's legs trembled as she stood. Her eyes were turned down, fixed on her child. "I just got here, sir!"

"What a pile of . . ." the man muttered. "There's usually lots of them here. Now, when you want to find them, there's not one of them around."

The patrol, their sharpened bamboo poles firmly in their hands, conferred among themselves. After a brief discussion they fanned out and began walking north toward the elephant grass. Soon they disappeared from view. On the railroad trestle, twenty meters to the south, a train appeared. A thunderous bellow followed it as it crossed over the river. A moment later the locomotive had disappeared, but from the direction of the station came the sound of the brakes clutching at the rail and then the cries of travelers.

Beside the right corner of the bridge a pair of shoes appeared: It was the unit leader, followed by a platoon commander, the village chief of Kaliwangan, and last, the district head of Karangjati. The group of men tramped down the hill to the place where the beggarwoman still stood beneath the bridge. The four men stopped, stared at the woman, and glanced around.

It was the district head who first addressed her: "Have you seen any male beggars around here?"

The woman trembled as she spoke; her eyes were fixed on the Japanese officer's sword. "I just got here, sir!" she cried before forcing her eyes from the sword and resting them once again on her child. She tightened her hold on the baby, bowed, and scurried away.

"This is where they usually are," the district head said, bowing respectfully to the Japanese officer.

The officer muttered something to himself in Japanese, then said to the others: "If we'd pulled them in last night, we might have him by now." He looked at the muscular Indonesian officer beside him. "What do we do now, Commander Karmin?" Karmin answered with a frown and a grunt. "Perhaps you have a new idea?" the Japanese officer asked.

Commander Karmin shook his head and looked at the village chief in disgust. "I said last night that his report was false." He turned back to the Japanese. "It could be this whole thing was in the chief's imagination." He gave the village chief an icy stare.

The chief's face lost its color. A wild fear filled his eyes as he looked at the Japanese officer. "No sir, no sir, it's true!" The man's hands trembled as he spoke. "I'm willing to swear, sir, that Hardo was in Kaliwangan last night. And that he was disguised as a beggar. I saw him myself, with my own eyes. For a quarter of an hour, maybe more. Maybe half an hour."

The Japanese officer narrowed his gaze as he looked at the village chief. His hands curled into fists. "You better watch it if you're lying."

The old chief's voice cracked as he spoke. "No, sir, I wasn't lying. It's the truth!"

"Is it?" the district officer asked, adding a new levy of pressure. "If it's true what you say, that you talked with him alone on a quiet road, then you should have captured him. But if you're only making trouble for the Japanese and the government," he warned, "you will have to pay the consequences. You are aware of that, aren't you?" He challenged the village chief with his eyes. "You understand, don't you?" he asked sharply.

The village chief's mouth moved automatically in silent prayer. He raised his hands in supplication. "I understand, I do, honored sir, but—"

"No buts about it!" the Japanese officer barked. The village chief swiftly bowed. "If you're making trouble for the Japanese, you'd better watch out!"

"But, but . . ." The village chief spoke quickly, afraid of being interrupted again. "When I met Hardo, I was on the road, at night. There was no one else around and I had nothing with me. How was I to hold him?" His hand clutched the guy wire as though it would give him strength enough to stand.

All eyes looked at Karmin as he spoke. "I suggest that we detain the chief until we find out what's really going on."

The village chief's eyelids fluttered hopelessly as he attempted to look at the Japanese officer. "I did, sir, I really did see him."

"You're not lying, are you?" the officer asked threateningly. "I've known Hardo a long time. I once came with him to your house. You remember that, don't you?" His bloodshot eyes bulged from lack of sleep. "You watch your step," he said shrilly.

"And how can you be sure it was even him?" the district head asked slowly.

"But I've known him for a long time, sir!" The village chief begged for confidence. "I'm not lying. Maybe now he's at—"

"Where is he at!" the Japanese officer demanded.

"At his father's, the former head of Karangjati district."

"You can stop your stories," Karmin advised the village chief. "Maybe you were seeing things when he appeared before you as a beggar." The village chief's head shook back and forth. Karmin now looked at his superior, the Japanese officer. "Sir, how about if we interrogate the village chief first?"

The Japanese paused in thought, muttered something, and then looked at the district head. "What about rounding up all the beggars?"

New blood suddenly surged through the village chief. His pale features glowed as he looked humbly toward the Japanese officer.

The district head gave a studied answer: "It would be hard to arrest them all. Why, there must be a hundred, maybe a thousand beggars in this city." The pallor returned to the chief's face once more.

"You're just lazy," the Japanese said with disgust. "Indonesia is a waste of our good money! If I turn you over to the military police, then you'll know what trouble is." Suddenly it was the district head who was pale. The officer slapped his hands on his hips and began to pace back and forth, finally stopping before the village chief, who seemed even more pale than before. "You!" The village chief released his hold on the steel wire and bowed. "If you are lying the military police will have your head. You got that? You do know that, don't you?" The village chief looked at Karmin for help but Karmin ignored him. "You know about the military police, don't you?" the Japanese screamed again. As the chief remained silent the Japanese grabbed the man's shirt with both his hands and began to shake him forcefully. "Do you? Do you?" The village chief kept his eyes on the ground. "Do you? Do you?" the Japanese officer continued to shout. His face grew redder and redder but still the chief said nothing.

As the Japanese officer's anger mounted he continued to throttle the village chief, whose head bobbed back and forth. Trembling and weak, the man was a lifeless puppet, swinging to the left and the right. When the Japanese finally released him, he stumbled backward, falling against the bridge pillar. Beads of sweat glistened on the officer's forehead; his face was a deep red. As he struggled for breath he glared hatefully at the district head. "So what about rounding up all the beggars?"

"That might produce results," the district head offered timidly.

"Then do it! Do it, you understand? Do you understand or not?" the officer pressed.

"I'll ask the police commissioner later to call his men together," he answered helplessly.

"Later? When?"

"Now, right away. I can telephone from the station," he said as he scurried away and disappeared around the right corner of the bridge.

The village chief was back on his feet again, stealing occasional glances at Karmin with a plea for help in his eyes. The Japanese officer fumed as he paced impatiently back and forth. His right hand gripped the leather handle of his sword. The sword's silver chain glistened in the light like the tips of breakers on the seashore. Karmin stood firmly in position but his eyes studied the old chief's dirty feet and his cheap homespun headcloth.

"That's it!" the Japanese cried with satisfaction. "We'll arrest them all." He approached the village chief again. "You're not lying, are you?"

"I'm not, I'm really not. Maybe he's . . ."

"Where?" Karmin asked impatiently.

"At his father's!"

"You're lying!" the Japanese officer barked. "His father is under arrest. I went to his house myself. And also to his hut in the field. So watch what you say!" His fist clenched, he struck the village chief's cheek with his left hand and then punched his nose with the right. The force of the blow bowled the chief backward. His head struck a pillar, and with his foot tangled in the guy wire, the village chief fell to the ground. "Don't lie to me. Don't ever lie to me!" His face was aglow as he stared at the chief kneeling on the ground below him. After the chief had struggled to his feet again, the officer snapped, "Where did you first meet him?"

"At my house," the village chief said with fright as he wiped his bleeding nose and mouth with his arm, turning his shirtsleeve to crimson.

"How long ago?"

"Three years."

The Japanese thought for a moment before studying the chief once more. Looking up at the span of the bridge, he mumbled something in his own language.

Commander Karmin stepped toward the village chief. "Don't bring anyone else into this," he advised. "If you do, you'll have to suffer for it later."

"But it's true, Karmin, I did talk with him last night," the village chief pleaded in despair. "What can I say? May I be struck dead as I stand here if I'm lying. And he told me, 'I want to go . . .'"

The Japanese officer quickly turned to the village chief. "Where was he going?"

"He said . . . he, he said that he wanted to go to the stars."

The officer's anger erupted again. "Are you making this up?"

"And then what did he say?" Karmin asked.

"That he would come to my house when . . ." The village chief struggled for an answer. His voice faltered as the Japanese officer stepped toward him.

"When?" the officer.

The village chief stepped back. "He said . . . he said

when the Japanese are defeated—" The officer's fist slammed into the man, knocking him to the ground. "Really, I'm not lying, sir," he moaned as he picked himself up again.

"Japan will not be defeated. You have been talking to enemy spies. Our military police will have your head!" The Japanese officer looked angrily at Karmin.

The smile that had been on Karmin's lips vanished. "Why didn't you try to trick him so that he could be arrested?" he immediately asked the village chief.

"I tried, Karmin," the chief answered honestly.

"How?"

"I offered him some clothes . . ." The Japanese officer kept his eyes on the village chief. He rolled up his sleeves and clenched his fists once more. "But—but he refused. Then I offered him five hundred *rupiah* to make him stay," the chief continued, "but he wouldn't take that either. And when I asked him where he was going, he said, 'I want to go to the stars.'"

The Japanese officer turned now to Karmin. "Does 'stars' have another meaning?"

"No," Karmin answered without pause.

The officer turned back to the village chief. "Who does he know in the area?" Still coughing and spitting blood, the old chief could not answer. The Japanese officer laughed at the sight. "Tell me," he insisted. The headman trembled with fright. "Who?" the officer demanded as he raised his fists in the air. "Who?" he screamed again before pummeling the chief once more.

Unable to defend himself, the village chief fell backward. Under a rain of blows he finally answered the question. "Ningsih! Ningsih!"

Hearing the chief's answer, Karmin swiftly turned his back to the men and walked a few meters away to lean against the sunlit pillar of the bridge.

The Japanese officer ended his attack. "Who?!" he asked again.

"Ningsih . . ." the village chief stuttered.

"Who is Ningsih!"

"My daughter," the headman moaned.

The interrogation ended as the Karangjati district head returned.

"Honorable Leader," the man addressed the Japanese officer, "I have conveyed your orders to the police commissioner. The auxiliary patrols have been ordered to round up all beggars and tramps."

The Japanese officer nodded to the district head, then looked back again at the chief. "Where is she?" he inquired.

"She teaches at the Darmorini School."

The Japanese officer looked at the district head. "Is there a teacher named Ningsih who teaches at the Darmorini School?"

The district head paused to think. "Yes, there is."

"There is, is there?"

The district head nodded. "Yes, there is."

The Japanese turned back to the chief. "Where does she live?"

The village chief's hand trembled as he pointed toward the southwest. "There," he whispered as his hand fell limply at his side.

Both the officer and the district head looked in the direction the village chief had pointed, but Karmin stared northward toward the bend in the river where the Lusi lost itself between the borders of bamboo. As elsewhere along the river, the embankment was dotted with cassava bushes and the ground littered with dry chocolate-colored bamboo leaves. None of the men beneath the bridge seemed able to speak and the village chief himself seemed to lack the courage to look in the direction he had pointed. Staring at Karmin's deep green boots, his eyes brimmed with tears.

"What about arresting the Darmorini teacher now?" the Japanese officer asked the district head.

Karmin coughed and stepped forward. "Honorable Leader," he said with deference, "to arrest a teacher in front of her students would not be good in Indonesian eyes."

"Not good?" The leader seemed displeased.

"No, not good at all," Karmin stressed. "It would have a bad effect on the students. They might begin to distrust all teachers."

The Japanese thought about this for a moment. "Then when can she be arrested?"

"After school, at her home. You may leave that up to me," Karmin said in a convincing manner.

The Japanese officer turned to the district head. "What do you think?"

"Yes," he nodded. "Maybe it would be best if Karmin questioned her first."

"What time does she come home?" the Japanese officer inquired.

Karmin shook his head. "When she does come home, I will arrest her, sir!"

The Japanese smiled and looked at the village chief, who was still spitting blood. "If you are lying, the military police will have your head!"

The village chief stared at the officer in horror. "I'm not lying, sir," he answered, terrified by his response. As he wiped his nose with his arm, the sleeve of his shirt grew even more red than before.

"I guess we can go then," the officer said, satisfied. "There are no beggars here." He turned to the district head. "Is there another place where beggars gather?"

"Leave that to me, sir."

The Japanese officer walked to the right side of the bridge, climbed the slope and disappeared. He was joined by the district head and then the village chief. Commander Karmin was the last to leave, his weary pace marked by dispiritedness and frustration.

Bright golden rays now danced on the tips of the bamboo, shedding more light on the area beneath the bridge. The damp leaves that littered the ground fluttered in the shallow wind and glimmered with the sun. On the opposite bank, a squad of auxiliary police was busy working its way through the wide fringe of grass. They stopped each man they met to check his right arm and continually shouted at people not to cross the river.

A quarter of an hour later an automobile roared to a stop before the bridge. A moment later, Karmin and the village chief of Kaliwangan clambered down the bank. Beneath the bridge they stopped. Karmin, a deep frown on his face, leaned against the pillar like a man drunk with uncertainty. Before him stood the frightened village chief, whose eyes were filled with fear.

Neither of them spoke at first, but finally the village chief's terror erupted. "God knows, Karmin, I didn't want any of this to happen." Karmin glared at the man and ground his teeth. "Really! I didn't want this to happen. I thought I was doing the right thing. Do you think I will be arrested?"

Karmin took a handkerchief from his breeches and wiped it across his face, mopping up the beads of sweat that glistened on his forehead, his nose, and his ears. His face was red as he returned the handkerchief to his pocket. "Yes," he replied.

The old man's head fell. "Prince in Heaven, help this old man! Oh, Karmin!" he cried out weakly.

Karmin's laugh mocked him. "What did you say? Me help you?" His upper lip was pulled tight. "How stupid do you think I am? Can't you see that even now you are under arrest?"

The headman's eyes pleaded for understanding. His mouth fell open as he gasped for breath and clutched his side. "Allah, my Prince!" He dropped to a sitting position on the ground and stared up at Karmin, his lips moving in silent prayer. Then he bowed again.

Karmin looked dreamily at the bend in the river, then shook his head weakly as if trying to change the course of his thoughts. He looked down at the old man, his eyes filled with disappointment, but said nothing.

"Will I be turned over to the military?"

"If Hardo's not caught, yes!"

"Oh, Allah! My daughter, my wife . . ." He hid his face behind his arm. "And will they cut my head off?"

"Yes!"

"Oh, Allah! Oh no, it can't be!" The village chief opened his arm. His red eyes glistened. "And Ningsih too?"

"Yes."

"Oh, Allah!" The village chief pounded his head with his hand. "Oh, why did this have to happen? Why?" He pulled himself up and clutched Karmin's arm. "Help me, please, help me!"

"Listen to me," Karmin said forcefully. "Until Hardo is caught you will be in the hands of the authorities. And Ningsih too. The Japanese officer said as much himself." Karmin pried the old man's fingers from his arm. "All I can tell you is to accept it. To place yourself in God's mercy and to pray that you and your family will be safe."

The old man permitted Karmin to free himself. His eyes traced the span of the bridge upward to the blue sky. He lifted his open palms to his ears and began to move his lips in silent prayer. As he prayed, his eyes showed a flickering of courage and acceptance.

"Sir," Karmin said. The village chief looked at him. "Why did you submit that report on Hardo?" Before the man could answer Karmin turned away to look at the bend in the river. "Isn't Hardo your future son-in-law? Isn't he your daughter's fiancé?"

"Oh, God, Karmin. You have no idea what this has done to me."

Karmin's eyes remained on the bend in the river. He spoke with a tone of regret: "I should have taken a stand a long time ago."

"What do you mean?"

"I don't know either why it has turned out like this." Karmin seemed to address his words to himself, as if unaware of the village chief's presence. "They're good men. No one can argue about that. They are good men."

"Who?"

Karmin looked back over his shoulder at the village chief. "Who else? Hardo and his friends."

"But, they're beggars!"

Karmin laughed bitterly. "And all beggars are bad?"

The old man evaded the question. "But Ningsih is a teacher."

"What do I care if she's a teacher or not? The point is she's faithful."

The old man shook his head and spoke softly. "But how would that be for my daughter, a teacher at Darmorini, to marry a beggar?"

Karmin looked back at the bend in the river and spoke to himself: "I wonder what they're doing now. How would it feel to be hunted down! To be on the run, trapped, hiding alone in a cave, living as beggars and now this?" He looked back at the village chief with disgust, and the old man bowed his head. "So you don't want Hardo for a son-in-law. Is that it?"

"He's a beggar . . ."

"Why didn't you say no to him before?"

"That's why I reported him. But now look at what's happened." He looked across the river at the opposite bank.

"So you would have the Japanese catch Hardo and the military police cut his head off. Would that make you happy?" The old man said nothing. "Ningsih is special—the only woman I know who has been completely faithful. If she were to hear Hardo had been beheaded . . ."

"Oh, God!" the old man cried, "I didn't know."

"Well I hope you're happy now!"

"God in Heaven, please don't scare me like this, Karmin. I didn't mean for this to happen. I didn't think anything like this would happen! I thought that when you came to my house it was because, because . . ."

"Because of what?"

The old man paused as if embarrassed. "I thought that you came to my house looking for Hardo because . . ." He looked at Karmin apologetically. "Because I had heard . . ."

"What had you heard?" Karmin stared at the old man. "What had you heard?" he asked again.

The old man bowed his head and scuffed the ground with his feet. "I can't tell you."

"What can't you tell me?" Karmin demanded.

"That, that . . ."

"What?"

"People said . . ." The frightened man stuttered. "People said that you'd had a falling out with Hardo and his friends."

"Is that what they said?"

The old man's fear seemed to subside. "Yes," he said with greater certainty. "And not just one person or two. Everyone in Blora was saying the same thing."

Now Karmin stuttered in embarrassed confusion. "Who told you that?"

"Why, everyone!" the old man answered.

Karmin sighed and looked around again at the bend in the river. He leaned despondently against the bridge. He seemed to address his words to someone who was not even there. "Who could have spread such a thing? Did they? Could they have done such a thing? Are the rumors true?" He closed his eyes for a moment, then pulled his head away from the pillar to look at the old man. "Did you really talk to Hardo?"

"Yes, for a quarter of an hour or more."

"About what?" Karmin turned his head to the left to listen to the whistle of a train. "The train to Rembang is pulling out," he murmured. "What did he say?"

"He said that he was going to the stars. I didn't know what he was talking about."

"That's all he said?"

"That and his promise to return. You know how Ramli and my wife are about Hardo. They begged me to find him and make him come home."

"Did he talk about me?" Karmin asked nervously.

"No. He said only that he would return after the Japanese have been defeated." Karmin ground the sole of his boot into the dirt. "Can you imagine saying such a thing? I can't. But—but the Japanese can't lose, can they?"

Karmin leaned his head against the pillar once more. Doubt lined his face and he drew a deep breath. "Did he say when that would be?"

"He told me to wait. He told me to go home and

wait. And he told me to give his regards to Ramli and my wife." Karmin continued to gaze at the bend in the river. "And when I came home without Hardo, Ramli sat there on his circumcision chair and stared at a photograph of Hardo until he fell asleep. His mother could do nothing to console him. That was when I wrote the report. I didn't even watch the shadow play or take the time to mingle with my guests." He seemed suddenly shocked. "Here we had a party for Ramli's circumcision and I didn't even know how to contact you. You said in the one letter you sent that you were going to be transferred but you didn't give an address." He paused before continuing. "You don't know what I was feeling inside. How do you think I'd feel if my daughter were to marry a beggar?"

As if reaching a decision, Karmin suddenly stood erect. "So then Hardo couldn't tell you when the Japanese will be defeated?"

"What he said was that 'people live for victory and then later live for defeat.' I won't forget those words." He asked more emphatically, "Can the Japanese be defeated?"

"That's right, man does not live for victory alone."

Neither man spoke as their eyes studied the ground. Both seemed to be following ghosts of their own memories. Both men frowned.

Reluctant to speak, the old man coughed, but then began the conversation once more. "Is there much of a chance that Hardo will be caught?"

"Is that what you want?"

"If he's not caught and the Japanese lose, he's going to come back one day to find me."

Resting the weight of his body against the pillar, Karmin sighed: "Yes." The look in his eyes prevented the headman from speaking. He sighed again. "People . . . people are often afraid of their own actions. That's normal, I suppose. But a person must have the courage to bear the consequences of his actions. Advice is cheap, I know, but the most difficult thing to do is to follow one's own advice. Even when it would be the best thing to do. So what's the use of worrying about whether or not Hardo comes back? Bear the responsibility for your actions." Karmin spoke more forcefully. "Listen to me. You're the one who's behind this commotion and I want nothing more to do with it. You can report what I've said; that's up to you. That is, if you want even more trouble."

The appearance of friendliness and calm that had softened the village chief's features now vanished, to be replaced by fear. "May lightning strike me down should I ever report you."

Karmin laughed sardonically. "If a person betrays another person once, who's to say he won't do it again, or again?"

"Trust me, Karmin! It was in your interest that I sent that report."

Karmin leaped toward the chief. "My interest?" he screamed. "What do you know about my interests?"

"Really, Karmin . . ." The old man tried to soothe the commander. "Once you're as old as I am, you too will be able to read the ways of young men." The old man's face shone for a moment. He moved his lips as if to speak but then tightened them again. A moment later he tried once more. "Given the way things turned out, there wasn't much I could hope for in Hardo. But say the Japanese lose and say Hardo comes back, if . . ."

"If what?" Karmin asked suspiciously.

"If you were to . . ."

"If I were to what?"

"If you were prepared . . ."

Karmin was growing impatient. "Whatever it is you're trying to say, I think it's about time you tell me.

You asked me to find a quiet place so that we could talk alone and that's what I did. So why can't you come out and say what you mean without wandering all over the place first? The unit leader is at the police station now but will be coming back here shortly. If you have something to say, then say it."

The old man's eyes asked for understanding. "Karmin . . . Ningsih, my daughter . . . I hope that you can help her."

"You got her into trouble without my help and I'm supposed to save her? You ignorant old fool! You should have know better! The Japanese never let their victims go." Karmin took a breath. "The trouble you've made for Ningsih, you've brought it on yourself and you must bear the consequences. Lift your head! Stick out your neck for the sword."

"But Karmin," the old man pleaded, "I did this for you, for your interests, to make a place for you."

"You keep talking about my interests! What the hell do you mean?"

"I thought that this way, with Hardo out of the way, you could take his place."

"God in heaven! Shut your mouth!"

The old man held tightly to the guy wire for support. His voice was almost a whisper. "But I thought that was what you wanted." He began to pray. "Allah, God the Most Powerful! How could I have misunderstood Your will? Oh, my Prince!" He rubbed his chest with his hand. His face was frozen. He groped in his pocket with his right hand. "I only meant well for you," he said earnestly. "I've saved up fifty thousand rupiah. I thought that someday you could have it. You can do whatever you want with the money if, if . . ."

"Keep your mouth shut!" Karmin shouted. The old man was silenced and did not interrupt Karmin as he spoke to himself. "People are saying that I betrayed them. I know that and everyone else knows too. No matter what, Indonesians will always be closer to other Indonesians than to the Japanese. I know why they blame me." He walked forward five steps, leaving the chief behind. He stopped and stood in place, his eyes on the curve of the river below. "I've sinned against them," he whispered. "I'm marked as a traitor. And what can I say? I thought that I was different, that I was a soldier nothing could move, that I would always stand fast for my beliefs. Why am I like this now?!" He turned toward the village chief to find him seated on the ground. "The Japanese will be defeated." He spoke with greater certainty now. "And I will return to you, Hardo. I'll look for you until I find you."

The old man stared anxiously at Karmin. "You won't tell him about what I did, will you?"

"You idiot! I'm sure he knows already. He knows who sent that report. I suppose you never thought about the possible effects of what you did, never imagined that they might turn on you. You listen to me. It's you who wanted Hardo out of the way and now you have to bear the consequences of your actions. Leave me out of it. If you don't have the guts to do that, then I suggest you look for him yourself until you find him and ask him for forgiveness. But . . ."

"But what?"

Karmin looked straight into the old man's eyes. "But he won't believe you."

"Then what can I do, Karmin?" he asked, afraid.

"What can you do?" Karmin asked lightly. "Nothing at all, because you're going to be sitting in jail. And then, in a couple of hours, the Japanese are going to come and take you way."

"No!" the old man cried and moved closer to Karmin. "You're just trying to frighten me, aren't you, Karmin?"

"No, I'm not."

The old man stared at the ground. "Won't you help me?" He seemed to be pleading for his life.

"What?" Karmin's tone was icy. "I am supposed to arrest you! I can't help you now. And talking like that, all you're going to do is to make matters worse."

"Are you angry with me?" Karmin did not reply; his attention was on the bend in the river. "Are you angry?" the chief asked again. Karmin sighed deeply. "Will Ningsih be arrested too?"

"I'll be arresting her later," Karmin answered bitterly.

"Oh no . . ." the chief moaned.

"Is this what you wanted to talk about? Have we finished?" Karmin didn't wait for an answer. "If you've had your say, then let's go."

"Where to?"

"The police barracks."

"Have mercy on me. I have a wife and children and you're going to hand me to the military? Oh, it's too much, it's too much! And Ningsih too. Have you no mercy for us at all?"

"Mercy is not for sale."

"But if the Japanese fall and Hardo comes back to take revenge. . . . Did they really arrest Hardo's father last night?"

"Yes, also the result of your actions!"

"Oh, this is too much!"

"Come on, let's go." The village chief was speechless as Karmin turned and walked away from him toward the right side of the bridge. There he looked back at the old man standing motionless below him, his eyes staring up at the edge of the span. "Come on! Get a move on!" Karmin called to him.

The old man mumbled sadly, "It's too much! Damn

them, damn them, damn them all." And then more slowly: "That was my last hope. Hardo's gone and now there's no hope from Karmin. That man punched my nose and made it bleed and no one even tried to help. I've been arrested. Now they're going to turn me over to the military and cut my head off. And Ningsih will be arrested too. Damn them! Damn them all! It's just too much!" Turning back to look at the river, he continued his mournful complaint. "And that son of a bitch Wong Tio Ham still owes me ten thousand. Damn him to hell too. With me in jail, he'll be having a good time with my money. And Haji Kalsum owes me two thousand. Damn him to hell. And just yesterday I bribed the district clerk with three thousand. Once he hears that I've been arrested is he going to smuggle any teak for me?" He went on in confusion and disbelief. "They're just trying to frighten me. No, they're not going to arrest me. Oh, son of a bitch!" he muttered. "You can't bribe the Japanese."

"Move it up!" Karmin shouted impatiently. The village chief stared back with heavy eyes. Karmin retraced his steps and pulled on the old man's arm.

The chief plodded along behind Karmin. "Am I really being arrested?" he asked.

"Yes."

"And Ningsih too?"

"Yes."

"Then why don't you just kill me and get it over with?"

The two men reached the side of the bridge. "I won't have to," Karmin said coldly, "The military police will do that. I'm not going to be the one to raise the sword over your head. Not I."

"Oh, my God . . . it's too much!"

They climbed the slope and disappeared from sight behind the upper corner of the bridge. Stillness was restored beneath the span.

FOUR

At two o'clock in the afternoon the heat in Blora is at its most intense. It is a grilling heat that chars the entire city. And in the front parlor of the house, the heat had taken its toll. The leaves of the flowers in their terra-cotta vase on the coffee table had curled and turned brown at their edges. Only the hidden leaves, those in the center of the arrangement, remained untouched.

Four low chairs of old teak, deep brown in color, were arranged around the coffee table. The four walls of the room, without a single painting or photograph to decorate them, were bare and creamy; they appeared to have been whitewashed only a few days before.

The front door to the parlor on the outside wall

faced the main street and the entrance to the station on the other side. The inner doorway that led into the house proper was in the opposite wall, and across it hung a curtain of rough mosquito netting. Two meters to the side of the front door was a window, its shutters open and its lower half covered with what once must also have been a mosquito net. Below the window and to the left was an escritoire; facing it, in the corner of the room, sat an armless chair with a thin pillow for a cushion. On top of the writing desk were two stacks of notebooks, each about twenty centimeters high, a pot of ink, a ruler, pencil, and fountain pen.

The curtain covering the back doorway opened and a young woman in traditional attire entered the room. Walking to the desk, she looked neither left nor right, and as she sat down on the chair, picked up the pencil, and began to inspect the notebooks.

After checking a few of the books on her right, she added them to the pile on her left. Putting down her pencil, she first looked at the window, then pulled the curtain aside. The expression on her face was serious as she stood and walked to the front door.

Commander Karmin walked into the room. "Ningsih," he said as he stopped before the young woman, wiping his forehead with a handkerchief. "How are you?"

"Fine," she replied as they sat down, facing each other on the low chairs. "You must be hot."

Karmin wiped the sweat from his brow once more, then put his handkerchief into his trousers pocket. "Yes, it's very hot."

"Karmin . . ." Ningsih hesitated. "Is it true that Hardo's here?"

"Where did you hear that?"

"Everyone is talking about him," she said sadly.

Karmin, who appeared to be in a daze, failed to answer. Seeing the trancelike look in his eyes, Ningsih lowered her head. Her voice betrayed anxiety. "It's not true, is it?" Karmin kept staring at her. With her head bowed, the young woman continued. "Everyone's been saying that. And they said that he has . . . that he has disguised himself as a beggar." She attempted to look at Karmin once more, but seeing the melancholy look in his eyes, lowered her gaze to the vase of flowers.

Slowly, Karmin's gaze too was drawn to the vase. "Yes," he said.

Ningsih emitted a short sigh. "The military raided this house last night. They said they were looking for someone but I didn't know who they wanted. It wasn't until this morning that I heard from my students that it was . . . that it was Hardo they were after." She eyed Karmin suspiciously. "And I suppose that's why you're here?"

Karmin, fixed in his seat, continued to stare at the vase of flowers. He said nothing, and with his left elbow resting on the arm of the chair, propped his head on his hand.

"Karmin?" she asked. Only now did Karmin look at her. "You don't seem to be yourself. Why do you look so sad?"

Karmin lifted his head and slowly took a deep breath. "I hope that this time you'll trust me, just this one time. After that, it doesn't matter; it's completely up to you." As he rose to his feet he looked tired and winded. "Don't worry, I'm not here to talk about that. I know you wouldn't want to anyway! All I'm asking is that just this one time you try to listen to me."

Ningsih frowned. "Please leave me alone."

"In God's name, no! Now will you listen to me or not?"

She glared at Karmin and pressed her lips tightly together. When she finally spoke, the words poured from
her. "I will not sit and listen to your pleadings, Karmin!
Whatever happened in the past is past and you will always be welcome in my home. But I never want to hear
you repeat those words again. It's just lucky that I have
brains enough to figure out what you're trying to say."
Karmin bowed his head. "So talk all you want, to your
heart's content, but remember," she warned him, "I
don't have to listen."

Karmin raised his head and stared at her with that
same wistful look in his eyes. "But Ningsih, believe me,
my intentions are only honorable," he pleaded softly.

Her smile seemed to mock him, but her tone was
friendly. "And what do you mean by honorable?"

"Will you listen?" he asked. She nodded. "I don't
like it that Hardo is on the run, a fugitive forever in dan-
ger of being caught." Ningsih smiled bitterly. "You
don't believe me, do you?"

"Isn't that what you wanted?"

"Then you too think I'm a traitor?"

Not answering him, she shifted her gaze to the entrance to the station. Her mouth was closed tightly as she
tried to catch her breath.

"You do," he stated. "And this is your punishment
for me?" Karmin spoke as if to himself. "Everyone says
I'm a traitor. But I never realized it. I never knew how
easy it was to be branded as such. They all think I'm a
traitor." He watched Ningsih silently as she studied the
station entrance. "You don't want to listen after all," he
sighed, turning his head to see what Ningsih was looking
at. "Ningsih?" he called softly. "Ningsih?" She turned
toward him. "What is it?"

"I guess you don't want to listen," he said, disheartened.

"And what am I supposed to listen to?"

"Just my voice. Listen to my voice," he replied hopefully. Only now did she begin to pay attention. "Maybe you can't see that what some people call betrayal might not always be the case." Ningsih smiled quizzically at Karmin's defense. "I've just learned for myself," he continued, "that public opinion has a life of its own. That public opinion, regardless of truth, is able to perpetuate itself. And this time I'm its victim. People are saying I'm a traitor. And let me tell you, I once saw with my own eyes, when the Dutch were on their knees, how people deal with traitors. There's no forgiveness. I know what it is when people speak of revenge. Now it looks like the situation might turn again and this time, I'll be the target of people's revenge." He stared at Ningsih, who now regarded him more seriously. "I once saw a man torn apart by a crowd because he was a traitor. So maybe the people will tear me apart too." He pulled his handkerchief from his pocket and mopped the sweat on his face. "But that's not what I'm here to talk about. What I'm trying to say is that sometimes a person doesn't realize he's been a traitor. That's what happened to me. I fully intended to keep the promise I made with Hardo and the rest of the men. I remember that night so well. The night we made our pact was moonless, and all we could see were stars flickering in the sky. And so that night we called for the stars to be our witness. We all promised to rise up simultaneously as soon as the rebellion in Blitar began. But then . . ."

Ningsih looked at him with pity in her eyes. The commander had lost his military bearing. "Then what happened?" she forced herself to ask.

"Two days before the rebellion was to begin, my fiancée married someone else. All of a sudden my future, the very reason for my existence, had disappeared. She was gone. What was there to fight for? I was supposed to fight the Japanese? Why? All I wanted to do was hide. I didn't keep my part of the promise." He lowered his head to his knees. "And Hardo, Dipo, and the rest became fugitives. I heard some had their heads cut off in Jakarta. And all that happened because I broke my promise. Not until later, after the consequences had grown and brewed into such a storm, did I finally realize that I was a traitor, that I had betrayed them." He fell silent, then looked at Ningsih with glassy eyes. "I am a traitor, whether I want to be or not!" He exhaled heavily. "Now will you trust me?" he asked sadly but hopefully.

Ningsih didn't answer his question. "That is why you're here?"

"No, it's something else. But not the subject that you won't discuss." He took off his cap and placed it on the table near the vase of flowers. "This is a sign, Ningsih. I take off my hat and raise it to you for your loyalty. You have remained loyal to Hardo, even though his life and future are uncertain. I won't try to test your loyalty again. Your loyalty makes me even more aware of my stupidity."

Ningsih laughed. "Where is Hardo now?"

"Good. You will listen," he said with relief. "Because I can't say anything if you ignore me like you usually do. But that's no surprise, considering how disgusting you must find me. Everyone knows I'm a traitor. You more than anyone else. But I've just realized that that's what everyone thinks. Do you believe me?" He looked at Ningsih, who nodded uncertainly. "I promise you I'm not lying! You must forget about what's happened." He clutched the back of his neck with his hands and placed his elbows on his knees. His eyes rested on his shoes. "Everyone knows who I am. Everyone is watching me. And when the situation changes—" His voice caught. "—I will not be able to escape. The people will have their revenge. The Japanese army is under pressure on every front and now the time has come; now is the most important moment in my life. And, I'm going to take a stand." He raised his head and looked at Ningsih. She looked over the platoon leader's shoulders and beyond him into the street. "Did you hear what I said, Ningsih?"

"Go on."

"I'm afraid you won't want to hear what I have to say."

"Go on," she said again, only now with her eyes on her guest.

"I came here to tell you that I am taking a stand. While it may allow me to escape from the people's verdict, it will mean my death at the hands of the Japanese. But I don't care anymore. I'm going back to Hardo. I'm going to find him and join him. I hope that my men will go with me. I'm serious, Ningsih. And if tomorrow or the next day I'm caught and have my head cut off, and if things turn out for you and Hardo, I hope that you'll tell him just this once for me . . ." He looked at her carefully. She listened intently.

"What is it that you want me to tell him?"

"That I'm sorry for not keeping my promise and that I will make amends." As Ningsih appeared to believe him he continued. "This time, the raid last night . . ." Karmin seemed unable to continue and paused to try another tack. "It's been very difficult for me this time to make sure that Hardo and his friends escape the raids. Oh, I'm sure they don't know what I'm doing or what I've done for them. I'm just as sure they wouldn't want to know. They probably have no idea that this time it wasn't me who betrayed them. And that this time it's going to be very difficult for them to escape. The fact is the traitor this time is someone who knows him very well."

"Who is it?" Ningsih asked quickly.

"Your father."

"Who?" she cried, jumping from her chair electrified. "How dare you say that about my father?" Her eyes widened as she jutted her chin out. Attempting to regain her composure, she spoke softly, but her eyes remained fixed on the road.

"Why do you think I kept asking you to trust me? And maybe you won't believe this either, but even now, at this very moment, you are under arrest."

She leaned weakly back in the chair and said in disbelief, "I am under arrest?" Her face went slack, all of her bravado gone. Her arms fell to the sides of her chair. She looked wearily at the commander and asked him slowly, "What have I done wrong?"

His reply was equally soft. "Nothing."

"Then why am I under arrest?"

"Until you say that you trust me, I cannot tell you. Do you trust me?" She didn't reply. "Just this once, won't you put your trust in me?" She straightened her back and glared at him. "I know how costly trust is," he went on. "I know how hard it is to give someone your trust, so I know how difficult it must be for you to trust me." His voice soothed her. "I admitted to being a traitor and now I beg you to listen. I will kneel on the floor before you if it would mean gaining your trust." He looked at Ningsih, disheartened. Her eyes were glazed and her face drawn with emotion. "Will you, Ningsih?"

"I'll try, Karmin."

"Only try?"

"I can't promise you anything more," she said. Her voice had gained new strength. "Go on."

"In a little while, a Japanese officer is going to come to the house—"

"What?" she cried. Her body stiffened and her face lost its color.

"He is going to question you. But don't be afraid. I'll do my best to make sure that you, Hardo, and his friends escape from your father's treachery."

"Karmin!" she screamed. "I'm trying to trust you but you keep dragging my father into this!"

"But it's true, Ningsih. Maybe you'd like to think it's a lie but it's not. Don't believe me if that's your choice, but it's not going to stop what is about to happen. Right now your father is being held at the police station."

"What did he do?" she asked anxiously.

He studied her carefully. She seemed to believe him now. "Last night Hardo visited your parents' home in Kaliwangan." Ningsih stretched back against the chair. "And for a quarter of an hour or more, out on the village road, he spoke with your father." She drew in a deep breath. Her brows arched as her eyes studied the top of the door. "After which, your father sent a report to the government—"

Ningsih jumped from her chair and stared at Karmin before yelling furiously, "My father?!" She stopped, then slowly lowered her body into the chair and leaned back once more.

"And because of his report the raids started again." He paused to add softly but seriously, "I was at the Cepu barracks last night when the telegram arrived telling us that Hardo had been seen in the Blora area. I went to my unit leader to convince him to take the job of finding Hardo out of the hands of the military police, and turn it over to me. That would have put me in charge of the

raids and so there wouldn't have been any worry. Fortunately, the leader of the military police has been tied up
for a week now in the Juana-Lasem area on the coast, so
there was little objection to my suggestion. But then
your father went and stirred things up—"

"My father?!" the girl cried again. "What did he do?"

"That report of his! And then, this morning too, beneath the bridge . . ." He turned slightly to point toward
the southwest. "That's where the Japanese beat him and
he confessed that you are Hardo's closest friend."

"My father . . ." she whispered in confusion. "So
that's why you're arresting me?"

"Don't be afraid! That I arranged too—I worked it
out so that you won't have to be taken to the police station. I lied to the unit leader in order to keep them from
arresting you at school. I wanted the chance to talk with
you first."

The girl studied his hat on the table. Karmin also
looked at his hat. Heavy moments passed before anything
more was said.

"What will they do to him?" Ningsih finally asked.

"He's just being detained."

"And Hardo, if he's caught?"

"I don't know."

"Will he be caught?"

"That I don't know."

"And what about me?"

"You're in my custody. Nothing is going to happen
to you," Karmin assured her.

"So why is the Japanese officer coming here?"

"To search your house," he answered quickly.

"But I haven't done anything." She seemed unable
to comprehend what was happening. She looked to the
left and right, studying the room, but once her eyes met

Karmin's she stopped. "What have I done?" she asked again.

"You've done nothing wrong," he stated. "But are you sure that Hardo is not here?" She shook her head weakly. "And you have no idea where in Blora he is?" She shook her head again. "Ningsih," he stressed, "I'm not here to interrogate you. That's not why I'm here. Please don't think that. I beg you to trust me." She nodded her head. "You've had no communication with him, is that right?"

She looked at him suspiciously, then shook her head hard. "No!" she said firmly.

"You have no letters?" he asked humbly.

"No!"

"Thank God. If you do, burn them immediately." He paused to think. "Do you have anything at all that might raise suspicion?" Her brow furrowed as she thought over the question. "I am not interrogating you," Karmin said again. "Is there?"

"No!" Her face relaxed again.

"Good. I believe you. So, when the officer comes, give him the same answers." She nodded. "You do believe me, don't you, that you're in my custody?" She did not answer but her eyes fell to his insignia. "No, Ningsih, I'm not one of those who are concerned with rank. I'm doing this only to keep Hardo from falling into the hands of the military. I know it's hard for you to believe me," he added weakly. "And I know that you and everyone else think I'm a traitor. But right now I need you to trust me. Will you, Ningsih?"

"Where is Hardo now?" she interjected, watching him carefully.

"Where?" he said dejectedly before he continued in disappointment. "Only God and Hardo himself know.

How am I supposed to know? The military police, the youth corps, and the men in my own platoon don't know where he is. And that's good, a good thing for him, that is. And even if I did know where he was, I wouldn't tell you. I just hope and pray that no one finds him."

"Do you think that he'll be caught?" Ningsih's voice trembled as she asked the question. "Isn't that a possibility?" She spoke as if afraid of the sound of her words, but slowly her calm returned and her eyes regained some of their brightness. She found herself finally able to look at the officer in front of her. He said nothing. She spoke with more strength. "Well?"

"As I said, only God and Hardo know!" He seemed irritated. "But you trust me, don't you?" He looked at Ningsih hopefully. "You do, don't you?"

"What does it matter?"

"Because I've made only trouble for you, Hardo, and his friends."

"Will you be satisfied if I do? Will that make you happy?" she asked.

Karmin nodded, ashamed. "Then you'll give me your trust?"

She thought for a moment, then spoke in a slow and sympathetic voice, "Karmin, you have my complete trust. I know that you regret your mistakes. But supposing you find Hardo, what will you do?"

"Don't ask me that!" he said and then fell silent. His forehead wrinkled as he peered up through his eyebrows. He heard something outside. "I hear an automobile. That must be the unit leader."

Ningsih silently tried to gather her strength. "What will he do to me?" she asked nervously.

"Don't worry. You aren't alone. You have me here to protect you." He was confident as he took his cap from the table and put it on. "I was right. That is the unit leader. You have no letters here, do you?" he asked as a reminder.

"No!" she answered, in a warm but nervous tone.

"If you do, get rid of them fast. And no other signs of communication, is that right?"

"None," she answered, warmer still.

Together they listened to the sound of the approaching automobile. They heard the squeal of brakes and then the skidding of tires on asphalt. Ningsih looked out the doorway toward the road. Suddenly, her face paled. Standing up, she whispered. "It's the Japanese. He's here!"

"Don't be afraid," Karmin told her. "He has the brains of a buffalo!" He looked over his shoulder. "It's the unit leader," he confirmed as he looked back at Ningsih. "Don't forget what I told you." Ningsih was as pale as before. "And don't forget my message for Hardo." The girl nodded dumbly. "Don't be afraid. There's no need to be afraid."

They heard the sound of boots treading on gravel and then the pounding of boots on the steps. Karmin faced the road outside, pulled himself into the proper military stance, and marched out of the foyer and onto the veranda. Ningsih pulled a chair to her side and stood beside it.

As the Japanese officer entered the room his eyes went directly to Ningsih. The young woman bowed her head deeply. Behind the officer were Ningsih's father, Karmin, and an Indonesian guard.

The Japanese officer stopped in front of Ningsih and pointed at her. His voice was stiff but not impolite. "Miss, you sit down please." The young woman took a few steps to sit in a chair that was farther away from him. The officer stepped forward to sit on the chair she had earlier occupied. He continued to stare at her. "Are you Miss Ningsih?"

"Yes, I am, sir," she answered with forced calm.

Karmin sat where he had been seated before. The village chief sat across from his daughter and the soldier stood stiffly in the doorway.

"Are you the daughter of this man?" The Japanese officer turned his head toward the village chief and then toward Ningsih. "Are you?"

"Yes, I am, sir," she answered slowly, stealing a look at her father. Her father's face was very pale. Blood stained his rumpled shirt.

The officer glared at the village chief. "And you, is this girl your daughter?" The old man raised his head slightly and nodded. The Japanese officer suddenly flushed and the tip of his nose turned red. "I want proper answers!" he growled. "Proper answers!"

"Yes, sir," the old man replied, trembling as he spoke.

"That's better!" the officer said as he released his right hand from the stock of his gun. He turned again to Ningsih. "Where is Hardo?" he asked courteously.

"I don't know," she answered calmly. Karmin, to her left, nodded.

"Is Hardo your fiancé, miss?" His voice was measured and polite.

"Yes, he is," Ningsih answered quickly. "But I don't know where he is," she hastened to add.

The Japanese officer looked at her sharply. "You will answer what I ask you, miss, and nothing more. Do you understand?"

Ningsih nodded but presented a challenge: "Please ask me anything you wish."

The Japanese officer blushed, but his voice retained its politeness. He looked from Ningsih to Karmin. "I trust Karmin," he said to her. "So I won't search your house myself."

"There is nothing here, Honorable Leader!" Karmin said at once.

"Do you have any idea where Hardo might be?" the Japanese officer asked softly. Ningsih appeared to ponder the question. "Do you?"

She shook her head. "No!"

"You do understand, miss, don't you . . ." The officer paused to begin again. "You must understand, miss, that if Hardo is not captured"—he looked at the bowed head of the village chief—"that your father will be handed over to the military." The headman's jaw trembled and his face twitched as all eyes turned toward him. "You do know the military police, don't you, miss? If Hardo is not caught, it will be your father's head.

Ningsih exhaled deeply, her courage leaving her body with her breath. She stole a glance at Karmin, a plea for help. Karmin shook his head. "I don't know," she said.

"And you too will be given to them," the Japanese threatened.

"I don't know," she repeated.

"And have your head cut off."

Another look at Karmin. Again he shook his head. "I don't know!" she insisted. At this response, the Japanese officer fell silent.

"I have questioned Miss Ningsih," Commander Karmin explained to his Japanese superior. "I questioned her very thoroughly." He looked directly at the man, then shook his head weakly. "But I found nothing incriminating at all."

The Japanese officer turned away from Karmin's gaze to look at the bowed figure of the village chief on his right. "Then we will continue to hold the village chief," he said sternly. The old man's head dropped further toward the floor.

"Why is my father being held?" Ningsih asked him.

"You don't speak, miss, unless you are spoken to. You say nothing!" The officer's voice was firm but controlled. He lifted his right index finger to his lips. "You say nothing."

Ningsih shook her head wildly. "You have to tell me why! What has he done?" She shook her head again but now much more weakly.

"Be quiet!" the officer snapped at her, his face turning red.

"I must know," she insisted.

"Silence!" the officer repeated. "Indonesians may not ask questions! You are Indonesian so you say nothing!" His fluency rapidly faded. "When Indonesian is with Japanese . . . with Japanese, you understand? No telling stories. You remember that." The man's eyes bulged as he spoke. "Indonesians no good. Indonesians must learn to keep their mouths shut. You understand? Do you understand?" Ningsih checked her anger. Her fear had vanished and along with it, the paleness of her features. Her cheeks glowed as she stared into the eyes of the Japanese. "Do you understand?" he asked her, receiving no reply. "Do you?" She still refused to answer. "You act smart with Japanese?" She remained fast in her silence, with her eyes still on the officer. Unable to hold her stare any longer, the officer finally bowed. "The village chief will be held," he reaffirmed. He looked at the old chief. "And if Hardo is not caught, the police will cut off his head."

The old man somehow managed to lift his chest. "I am not lying, sir. I told you the truth. He was here." He searched for his daughter's eyes but when their eyes met, he immediately looked down again. "I am not lying," he repeated.

Karmin looked at Ningsih, his eyes pleading for her trust. Ningsih inhaled deeply and for a moment the air in the room seemed calm. As the guard at the doorway shifted his weight, all eyes turned momentarily toward him. The tension seemed to subside.

"And you will be held too, miss. Until when, I don't know," the Japanese officer added. "Maybe a year, maybe ten years, maybe your whole life."

Ningsih demanded an answer. "What have I done wrong?"

"You have connections with a traitor."

Shock appeared on the girl's face. "Where is your proof?"

"Your fiancé is a traitor."

Tears welled in Ningsih's eyes as she sought help from Karmin. Karmin shook his head. "That's no proof," she stammered.

"But you will be held," the officer reaffirmed.

As Ningsih fell silent the tension returned. For each of the occupants the rumble of the train from Rembang now pulling into the station was a distinct roar. The riot of voices and sounds from the travelers rushed the house and entered inside. The small group in the room listened to the neighing of horses and the jingling of the bells that decorated them as they pulled their carts along the streets. They heard troops singing in Japanese, a song that was interrupted by sporadic cheers and shouts.

They listened again. They heard a shout. "Hooray! The Volunteers and army have been disbanded!" And then they heard more shouts: "Hooray! Hooray! Hooray!"

"What's that?" the officer muttered in Japanese before standing and roughly pushing his chair aside with his feet. He walked to the doorway and looked outside to the left and right.

Karmin listened more carefully to the voices. Beads of sweat glistened on his face. He leaned to his right, placing his mouth near Ningsih's ear. "The Volunteers and army have been disbanded," he whispered. "That's what they're screaming."

"But why?" she whispered back.

"Japan has probably been defeated."

The faces of the two young people glowed; the eyes of Ningsih's father glazed over as he stared at them. Suddenly aware that someone was watching him, Karmin quickly straightened his body.

"What's happening, Karmin?" the old man asked.

The sound of the village chief's voice caused the Japanese officer to turn around. He stared at the three suspiciously. The village chief swiftly bowed his head again. Ningsih tapped her wooden sandals on the floor. Karmin took out a handkerchief, wiped his face, and then returned the handkerchief to his pocket.

Slowly, like a cat spying its prey, the Japanese officer returned to his chair and sat down. His eyes moved from one person to another, each time growing wider with suspicion. Finally, he fixed his eyes on Karmin. He could check his curiosity no longer. "What's happening?" he asked.

Without answering the question, Karmin rose and walked to the door, with the eyes of the Japanese officer following his movements. The man's suspicion was mounting. At the doorway Karmin listened more carefully. The crowd outside continued to shout. Karmin turned and looked back at the Japanese officer. "Have the Indonesian volunteers and army been disbanded?" he asked. His superior appeared not to hear. "What does this mean, sir?" Again receiving no answer, he turned and left the room.

As the noise outside increased, the occupants of the

room listened more carefully. The cheers and shouts of adults were followed by the laughter of numerous children.

Karmin came back to the room, his face now deep red, and dropped into his chair. "Honorable sir . . ." He seemed mystified. "Almost all of the men out there are volunteers from our battalion." The Japanese officer blanched. "They said that our battalion has been disbanded too. What does this mean?"

Ningsih looked at Karmin carefully, as did her father. The officer scratched the back of his neck as if unsure of what to do.

"We'd better go to the battalion," Karmin suggested. "Men from the other platoon said that my platoon is the only one that has not yet been disbanded. What does this mean, sir?"

The officer thought for a moment before replying firmly, "We will look for Hardo until he is caught." He glared at Ningsih, who immediately paled. "After that we will go back to the battalion. But traitors will be punished first!" He looked at the village chief. "You will be released only after this matter is settled. And if you have lied, if you have lied to the Japanese, your head will fall." He paused and then, like a madman, jumped up and ran to the door. Laughing wildly, he disappeared. Karmin also jumped from his chair and rushed outside with the guard. On the veranda, the Japanese officer was still laughing.

Ningsih rose to follow, but her father stood to hold her. In his clumsy embrace, she stared at her father and asked him, "What's happening?"

"Oh, my little girl, such trouble I've caused you. But now you're free." Tears of happiness ran down his cheeks.

"What's happening?" she repeated, rigid in her father's arms.

"And I'm free too!" the chief laughed. "The Japanese won't have my head after all."

Unable to return her father's embrace, Ningsih let her eyes wander to the desk in the corner of the room. Her father held her tightly by her shoulders. "Why are you doing this?" she finally asked.

"Don't you understand?" he almost screamed. "You're safe! You're safe. And I'm safe too." He gazed at his daughter. "I just saw him."

Ningsih finally began to yield to her father, but her eyes remained on her desk. "Father," she whispered, "what did you do?"

The old man drew a sad breath. "It was for you . . . it was all for you that I did it." He loosened his hold to stand beside her. "I'm free, Ningsih! And you're free too. I saw him. And we're rich, Ningsih! We're rich. Let's go home."

Neither of them spoke for a moment. From outside came the sound of the crowd and the laughter of the Japanese officer.

"Let's go home, Ningsih!" her father beckoned.

"Home? But we're under arrest!"

"No, we're not. We're free now. So let's go home. They've caught him. We can go home!"

"Who has been caught?" she inquired quietly.

"Why, Hardo, of course."

"Hardo?" Ningsih's body went stiff. Her face paled. "How do you know?"

"I saw him! I saw him under guard."

Ningsih ran to the door. Her father followed slowly behind.

The room was quiet once more. The flowers in the vase fluttered softly in the light wind. Outside, on the veranda, the air was filled with laughter and cheers.

The Japanese unit leader stood on the veranda, hands on his waist, flanked on his left by Commander Karmin and on his right by the military police commissioner. In front of him, near the stairway, stood the district head of

Karangjati, whose face was red from the heat. Below him, in front of the veranda, a patrol squad stood guard over three beggars: Hardo, Dipo, and Kartiman.

"We caught them near the bridge," the district head said proudly as he pointed in the direction of the Lusi bridge. "Right near the place where we had been talking earlier." He then turned toward the station and looked at the three beggars and the watchmen sweltering in the sun.

The laughter of the Japanese officer caused his chin to shake and his teeth to protrude sharply. "At last, at last," he cried with delight. He gestured with his right hand and the patrol led the beggars to him. "So you were trying to play games with the Japanese, were you? Well, were you?"

The beggars maintained a military stance, chins out and eyes focused directly forward. The district head moved to the side in search of shade but the patrol remained standing beneath the hot sun.

The commissioner turned around, his right hand gripping the butt of his pistol. "Step forward!" he shouted but the three beggars remained in place. "Forward!" he repeated, but again with no success. He glanced at the Japanese officer. "Is this the one?" he asked, pointing at Hardo. "There's a scar on his right arm."

"Put your arm out!" the officer ordered.

Hardo clenched his jaw and stuck out his arms. The Japanese officer stared at them. The sound of Dipo grinding his teeth caused everyone to turn toward him.

Something seemed to twitch inside the Japanese. "Dipo!" he shouted before scouring Kartiman with his eyes. "And Kartiman!" he screamed, and laughed wildly again. "This is good, very good," he said. "Very good indeed."

A crowd began to gather around the gate in the fence. Passing carts slowed their pace for their drivers to peer at the veranda. Above the station across the street, the Japanese flag, the Rising Sun, waved in the breeze.

"So Indonesians are traitors, huh?" the Japanese said to Hardo as both an insult and a challenge. "You will be sent to Jakarta to have your head cut off. You like that, huh?"

Hardo smiled and lowered his arms. Looking beyond the Japanese officer, he found Karmin at the officer's back. He nodded almost imperceptibly, at which Karmin lowered his eyes. Continuing his search, Hardo found Ningsih and her father with his arms around her. He glanced at the police commissioner and smiled again.

"So, you are not afraid?" There was pleasure in the officer's voice. "You're not afraid of the military police?" He stepped toward Hardo and clenched his hands as if ready to fight. "You're not afraid of the sword?" Hardo smiled. The Japanese officer poised himself to strike, but suddenly his body went rigid. He swayed stiffly as his eyes wildly searched the scene around him.

Beyond the crowd at the gate a truck proceeded slowly down the street. A man standing on top of the truck shouted through a megaphone. "Indonesia is free! Indonesia is free! Japan has surrendered to the Allies!"

For a moment all action was suspended; the crowd became a frieze. Then the patrol, with their bamboo spears standing before them, turned together toward the sound of the voice.

The truck was in front of the house, the man atop it still shouting through his megaphone. He turned the megaphone in their direction. "Japan has lost. Japan has surrendered to the Allies. We are free! Sukarno and Hatta have proclaimed independence!"

The truck moved slowly eastward. As it disappeared from sight, all eyes turned to the bloodless face of the Japanese officer. Shoulders drooping, the man gazed in shock at the Japanese flag fluttering above the railway station.

A crowd of schoolchildren ran dancing through the street, shouting in unison, "Japan has surrendered. Indonesia is free! Japan has surrendered. Indonesia is free!" The crowd of people who had been staring at the Japanese now turned their eyes to the flag above the station. A great shout erupted. "Tear that damn flag down!" Even as the cry faded, the Rising Sun, which had waved so proudly there for three and a half years, began to fall to the ground. The fingers of those who tore at the rope sparked with hate, and the Japanese officer grew more ashen as he watched the flag's ignominious descent. When it had finally disappeared from sight the officer raised his eyes again, slowly tracing the black and white flagpole to its now naked top. "Indonesia is free! Indonesia is free!" The cry came again, followed by a resounding chorus of cheers. Ningsih and her father emerged from the doorway of her house.

The faces of everyone except the Japanese officer were flushed. The crowd was drunk with emotion. Dipo suddenly clenched his fists, raised them high above his head, and screamed, not a battle cry, but "Freedom! Freedom! Freedom!" At that moment the Red and White, the new nation's flag, rose gracefully up the pole.

The unit leader flushed, his pallor becoming crimson. He bowed his head as if in prayer. In front of the station on the street people were screaming and shouting. The gate was thick with people staring at the officer, the defeated Japanese, and his prisoners. The Japanese officer moved his hand to his gun and tore it from its holster. His eyes flashed with fury. He threw back his shoulders, jerked open the catch of his gun, and began firing into the crowd. People screamed and scattered in panic, even the policemen who had been guarding the prisoners.

When a moment later the burst of the automatic stopped, Karmin jumped forward and grabbed the officer's arm. Trying to free himself, the officer bent his body and curled his arm downward. He spread his feet to find his balance. The men stooped and wrestled in position. The area around them had cleared except for the commissioner and the district head, who lay cringing on the veranda floor with their hands over their heads. Hardo stood by passively as the two men fought. Kartiman stood too, surprised to have escaped from the blast of gunfire. Dipo walked calmly to where the men were fighting and drew the officer's sword from its sheath at his waist.

The fight continued. The Japanese bent lower, curling the gun between his legs. Suddenly it went off again.

"Drop it!" Dipo screamed as he pressed the tip of the sword into the officer's back.

"Mercy!" he screamed. Karmin pulled the gun from his hands. As blood began to cover the back of the officer's shirt, he screamed again, "Have mercy, Indonesian!" He gasped for breath. "Indonesia is free!" he shouted hoarsely. "Long live Indonesia."

The officer's bodyguard, frozen in the corner, suddenly awakened from his spell. He approached the commissioner and the district head, who picked themselves up from the floor, their faces drained of color and their bodies trembling.

Dipo screamed at the officer, "On the ground!"

"Have mercy, Indonesian! Forgive me," he cried even as he knelt on the floor. His breath came in spurts. His face was colorless as his blood oozed over the back of his shirt.

On the street, the patrol came running back toward the house, their bamboo spears in hand. Felled by the officer's gunfire, four bystanders lay writhing in pain at the gate.

They groaned miserably as they were lifted and carried away. Above the station the Red and White waved proudly in place of the Rising Sun. More men came running, many of them with guns, and crowded into the yard.

The officer's body shook. "Let me live, Indonesian. Mercy!" he cried again.

The crowd hoisted their weapons and shouted, "Give him to us!"

Dipo swung the shining sword through the air and toward the officer's neck. He was weak and without the control he had once had; the sword missed the officer's neck completely and skimmed the top of his head. Knocking off the officer's hat, the sword clipped the crown of his skull and slammed into the floor. In the middle of the officer's head was now a palm-sized patch of white. A moment later the white turned red. As the officer fell silently to the ground his blood began to run from the wound and spread across the floor.

The men in the yard stared in silence as they slowly lowered their weapons. Hardo and Kartiman looked at each other. The district head covered his eyes with his hands and turned toward the wall. His shoulders heaved as he began to vomit. Near him the police commissioner clung desperately to the post of the veranda, trying to hold himself erect.

Dipo stared at the jagged piece of scalp and brain on the floor beside the corpse, a strange island in a pool of red blood. In his hand hung the sword, his immobile fingers on the handle and its tip on the floor. He turned and stared at Karmin, his eyes blazing with hate. Karmin approached him and handed him the officer's gun. He then stood at attention directly in front of Dipo.

The crowd in the yard began to shout: "Commander Karmin is a traitor!" The cry soon became a roar. There came another cry: "Give him to us!" And then another cry, this one louder still: "We want his hide!" Bamboo spears danced over people's heads. With their ends covered in oil, the spears glistened in the light. The shouts grew louder still.

Hardo walked to the front of the veranda and stared sadly at the crowd. The chains that bound his wrists clattered as he lowered his arms. The crowd moved forward with their spears waving above them. Hardo raised his hands, and slowly lowered them again. The shouts faded.

For a moment there was silence, but a moment later the cries began again. "Give us the police commissioner, the district head, and Commander Karmin. They are traitors! Give them to us, Hardo. We will have their blood."

In the corner of the veranda the district head leaned against the wall, his legs buckling under him. His mouth gaped, his eyes were half open as he tried to control his breathing. The police commissioner swayed back and forth like a small boat hit by a wave, and then slumped to the floor against the wall.

In the yard the dancing spears seemed to multiply and unite. The crowd moved forward. Hardo raised his hands again, this time to shoulder height, as if to stay a tumbling wall. His eyes were still glazed, his jaw clenched, and his chin thrust downward. The crowd quieted and fell back a step.

With his left hand Dipo lowered the gun to the floor and placed his right foot on it. He stared at Karmin and ground his teeth. He was a cat ready to strike its prey, but afraid at the same time another cat might make the kill first. "Karmin!" he snarled.

Karmin righted his stance and saluted. "Yes!" he answered in Japanese.

"On your knees!" Dipo ordered.

"Yes!" he said and dropped to his knees.

Dipo stepped forward, his eyes on the silver sword

in his hand. When he rubbed the back of Karmin's neck the crowd roared its approval and stepped closer.

Hardo kept his hands in the air. "Stay back!" he screamed but the crowd ignored him. Their attention was on Dipo, who was pressing the shoulder of his prey. Their eyes gleamed like those of hungry jackals. Their cries rose and mingled: "Go ahead, Dipo, do it! No mercy! Cut off his head! Give him to us, Dipo! We'll do it for you!"

Hardo looked back at Dipo to see him with the sword raised over his head. Below him, on the floor, Karmin bowed, neck out, ready for the sword.

"Dipo!" Hardo cried.

The sword hung motionless in the air. When Dipo looked back at Hardo, hate filled his eyes. He ground his teeth together. He looked deranged as his mouth dropped open and his jaws moved up and down. He gasped for breath. His bloodshot eyes begged for more blood. He blinked and scowled, but his body remained immobile. Suddenly he opened his mouth and screamed "Damn you!" Throwing the sword down, he walked to the front of the veranda and down its steps. As he entered the jackal-eyed crowd, the dancing spears swayed as he wove his way through.

With Dipo's departure Hardo looked back at Karmin. "Stand up," he told him. Karmin pulled himself up and stood at attention before Hardo, ready to salute.

The crowd moved forward again. "Traitor! Traitor!" they screamed. "Karmin is a traitor. Give him to us!"

"Silence!" Hardo shouted back, but the crowd was no longer willing to listen and screamed even louder. "Get back!" Hardo cried with all his strength even as the crowd took another step forward. Their bamboo spears merged into one. Hardo gazed back at Karmin. "Run! Go out the back door."

Instead Karmin leaped in front of Hardo to stand at

the edge of the veranda. The crowd surged forward again with a crest of spears waving over their heads.

Hardo pulled on Karmin's shoulder. "Quick! Run!"

Karmin looked straight into the crowd and their hungry eyes. The movement forward ceased and the cries and shouts faded as Karmin threw off his jacket and stripped himself of his shirt and jersey. As if suddenly bewitched, the crowd stood still. Karmin stood before them, baring his naked chest. He unhitched his officer's belt and threw it on the floor.

"Please!" Hardo begged. "Get out of here!"

But Karmin advanced another half step. Lifting his officer's cap he threw it through the air and into the crowd. "Kill me!" he shouted at the crowd. "Kill me! I am a traitor!"

The crowd stood mesmerized. The dance of their weapons slowly came to a halt and one by one were lowered to the ground.

"Kill me!" he demanded. "I am Platoon Commander Karmin. I am a traitor!" He advanced another step to stand directly before the crowd, only an arm's length away. "Come on! Kill me!" He challenged each of them with his eyes and soon each of them bowed their heads.

"Karmin . . ." Hardo begged.

But Karmin didn't look back. He screamed again. "Here I am—Commander Karmin. Kill me!" The crowd did nothing. "Why won't you kill me?" He raised his arms. "Don't you want to kill me?" he asked. "Don't you want to?"

Now Hardo shouted at the crowd. "Go home, all of you. Go home!"

They all looked up at Hardo but then bowed their heads again. The crowd began to disperse. People left silently with their heads down. Soon the crowd was gone.

At a distance most turned to look at Hardo and Karmin but then turned and walked on again.

"Karmin . . ." Hardo said.

Karmin stared at his officer's hat lying crushed and crumpled in the yard but then, as if startled, he spun around and looked at Hardo. "Yes!"

Hardo offered his scabby hand and Karmin took it in his own. They walked together toward the door, but there they were halted by the sight of the village chief bent over his daughter, Ningsih.

"Oh, my girl. Oh, my God, my little girl" he wailed, his tears rolling down his cheeks and his body racked by sobs.

Hardo bent down to see Ningsih covered in blood. A bullet from the Japanese officer's gun had entered her chest, risen at an angle, and lodged in her back. Her eyes were clouded. Hardo grabbed her by the shoulders and shouted, "Ningsih, Ningsih!"

"Who are you?" she whispered inaudibly.

"Don't you know me?" he stuttered.

She shook her head weakly. "Leave me be." Her breathing was irregular. "Let me die in peace . . . I have my memories." Her lips stopped moving. Her eyelids twitched and then were still. Her mouth opened slightly. Finally, and only then, her breathing stopped.

The old man screamed like a monkey in a trap. Hardo stared at the bullet hole in Ningsih's chest and her blood as it oozed from the hole. Karmin stood nailed to the floor. The district head, the police commissioner, the Indonesian guard, and Kartiman gathered around.

Hardo heaved a heavy sigh.

Bukit Duri Prison, 1949